THE GAN-FINN

Weird Tales from Northern Seas

Second Printing

Norwegian Legends

by Jonas Lie
Illustrations by Laurence Housman

Penfield
BOOKS

Jonas Lie
(1833-1908)

Born near Oslo, Jonas Lie and his family lived in Tromsø until he was twelve years old. His father was a district judge. Life in this rugged Land of the Midnight Sun inspired his work in telling the tales and traditions of the Arctic lands. He attended the Naval Academy for six months, and his passion for the sea is evident in much of his writing.

Lie became a lawyer and bank commissioner in Oslo, but after the financial crash of 1868, he decided to become a full-time writer, and quickly became the toast of Scandinavia and Europe for his novels. His works were translated into German, English, Japanese and other languages. He received the King Oscar II Medal of Merit in gold and a government author's stipend for life. His works include *The Commodore's Daughters; The Family at Gilje; A Norse Love Story: The Pilot and His Wife; The Slave of Life; The Visionary; Ole Bull,* a biography of the violinist; *Trolls I* and *Trolls II, Merry Wives,* a play; *When The Iron Curtain Falls; The Ulfvungs,* and many others.

Weird Tales was written originally in Danish. The official language in 19th century Norway was Dano-Norwegian, as Denmark had dominated Norway for four centuries. Linguistic reforms in the early 20th century did not produce a Norwegian language for all the people in the country. The Norwegian language today has a Danish influence and regional dialects.

—Joan Liffring-Zug, Publisher

Acknowledgments
Edited by Robin Ouren and Jean Caris-Osland,
Dorothy Crum, Joan Liffring-Zug, Miriam Canter, Georgia Heald, and Greta Anderson
Research assistance by Carol Hasvold, Registrar -Librarian, Vesterheim, the Norwegian-American Museum.
Graphic Design by Robyn Loughran, Dana Lumby, and Kathy Timmerman

First printed 1893
ISBN 1-932043-41-1
Library of Congress Control 2007 924294

PREFACE

Jonas Lie is sufficiently famous to need but a very few words of introduction. Ever since 1870, when he made his reputation by his first novel, *"Den Fremsynte,"* he has been a prime favorite with the Scandinavian public, and of late years his principal romances have gone the round of Europe. He has written novels of all kinds, but he excels when he describes the wild seas of Northern Norway, and the stern and hardy race of sailors and fishers who seek their fortunes, and so often find their graves, on those dangerous waters.

Such tales, for instance, as *"Tremasteren Fremtid,"* *"Lodsen og hans Hustru,"* *"Gaa Paa!"* and *"Den Fremsynte"* are unique of their kind, and give far truer pictures of Norwegian life and character in the rough than anything that can be found elsewhere in the literature. Indeed, Lie's skippers and mates are as superior to Kjelland's, for instance, as the peasants of Jens Tvedt (a writer, by the way, still unknown beyond his native land) are superior to the much-vaunted peasants of Bjornstjerne Bjornson.

But it is when Lie tells us some of the wild legends of his native province, Nordland, some of the grim tales on which he himself was brought up, so to speak, that he is perhaps most vivid and enthralling. The folklore of those lonely subarctic tracts is in keeping with the savagery of nature. We rarely, if ever, hear of friendly elves or companionable gnomes there. The supernatural beings that haunt those shores and seas are, for the most part, malignant and malefic. They seem to hate man. They love to mock his toils, and sport with his despair.

In his very first romance, *"Den Fremsynte,"* Lie relates two of these weird tales (numbers 1 and 3 of the present selection). For another tale, in which many of the superstitious beliefs and wild imaginings of the Nordland fishermen are skillfully grouped together to form the background of a charming love story, entitled "Finn Blood," I have borrowed from the volume of *"Foraellinger og Skildringer,"* published in 1872.

The remaining eight stories are selected from the book *"Trold,"* which was the event of the Christmas publishing season at Christiania in 1891. Last Christmas a second series of *"Trold"* came out, but it is distinctly inferior to the former one.

R. Nisbet Bain
1893

TABLE OF CONTENTS

The Fisherman
and the Draug

On Kvalholm, down in Helgeland[1], dwelt a poor fisherman, Elias by name, with his wife Karen, who had been in service at the parson's over at Alstad. They had built them a hut here, and he used to go out fishing by the day about the Lofotens.

There could be very little doubt that the lonely Kvalholm was haunted. Whenever her husband was away, Karen heard all manner of uncanny shrieks and noises, which could mean no good. One day, when she was up on the hillside, mowing grass to serve as winter fodder for their couple of sheep, she heard, quite plainly, a chattering on the strand beneath the hill, but she dared not look over.

They had a child every year, but that was no burden, for they were both thrifty, hard-working folks. When seven years had gone by, there were six children in the house, but that same autumn Elias had scraped together so much that he thought he might now venture to buy a *sexæring*[2], and henceforward go fishing in his own boat.

One day, as he was walking along with a *kvejtepig*[3] in his hand, and thinking the matter over, he unexpectedly came upon a monstrous seal, which lay sunning itself right behind a rock on the strand, and was as much surprised to see the man as the man was to see the seal. But Elias was not slack; from the top of the rock on which he stood, he hurled the long heavy *kvejtepig* right into the

1. *Helgeland*: A district in northern Norway.
2. *Sexæring*: A boat with three oars on each side.
3. *Kvejtepig*: A long pole, with a hooked iron spike at the end of it, for spearing Kvejte or halibut.

monster's back, just below the neck.

The seal immediately rose up on its tail right into the air as high as a boat's mast, and looked so evilly and viciously at him with its bloodshot eyes, at the same time showing its grinning teeth, that Elias thought he should have died on the spot for sheer fright. Then it plunged into the sea, and lashed the water into bloody foam behind it. Elias didn't stop to see more, but that same evening there drifted into the boat place on Kvalcreek, on which his house stood, a *kvejtepole*, with the hooked iron head snapped off.

Elias thought no more about it, but in the course of the autumn he bought his *sexæring*, for which he had been building a little boat shed the whole summer.

One night as he lay awake, thinking of his new *sexæring*, it occurred to him that his boat would balance better, perhaps, if he stuck an extra log of wood on each side of it. He was so absurdly fond of the boat that it was a mere pastime for him to light a lantern and go down to have a look at it.

Now as he stood looking at it there by the light of the lantern, he suddenly caught a glimpse in the corner opposite, on a coil of nets, of a face which exactly resembled the seal's. For an instant it grinned savagely at him and the light, its mouth all the time growing larger and larger; and then a big man whisked out of the door, not so quickly however, but that Elias could catch a glimpse, by the light of the lantern, of a long iron-hooked spike sticking out of his back. And now he began to put one and two together. Still he was less anxious about his life than about his boat; so he then and there sat himself down in it with the lantern, and kept watch. When his wife came in the morning, she found him sleeping there with the burnt-out lantern by his side.

One morning in January, while he was out fishing in

his boat with two other men, he heard, in the dark, a voice from a skerry at the very entrance of the creek. It laughed scornfully, and said, "When it comes to a *femböring*[4], Elias, look to thyself!"

But there was many a long year yet before it *did* come to that; but one autumn, when his son Bernt was sixteen, Elias knew he could manage it, so he took his whole family with him in his boat to Ranen[5], to exchange his *sexæring* for a *femböring*. The only person left at home was a little Finn girl, whom they had taken into service some years before, and who had only lately been confirmed.

Now there was a boat, a little *femböring*, for four men and a boy, that Elias just then had his eye upon—a boat which the best boat builder in the place had finished and tarred over that very autumn. Elias had a very good notion of what a boat should be, and it seemed to him that he had never seen a *femböring* so well built *below* the waterline. *Above* the waterline, indeed, it looked only middling, so that, to one of less experience than himself, the boat would have seemed rather a heavy goer than otherwise, and anything but a smart craft.

Now the boatmaster knew all this just as well as Elias. He said he thought it would be the swiftest sailer in Ranen, but that Elias should have it cheap, all the same, if only he would promise one thing, and that was, to make no alteration whatever in the boat, nay, not so much as adding a fresh coat of tar. Only when Elias had expressly given his word upon it did he get the boat.

But "yon laddie"[6] who had taught the boatmaster how to build boats so cunningly *below* the waterline—*above* the waterline he had had to use his native wits, and they were scant enough—must surely have been there before-

---

4. *Femböring*: A large boat with five oars on each side, used for winter fishing in northern Norway.
5. *Ranen*: The chief port in those parts.
6. *"yon laddie"*: *Hin Karen* = "the devil."

hand, and bidden him both sell it cheaply, so that Elias might get it, and stipulate besides that the boat should not be looked at too closely. In this way it escaped the usual tarring fore and aft.

Elias now thought about sailing home, but went first into the town, provided himself and family with provisions against Christmas, and indulged in a little nip of brandy besides. Glad as he was over the day's bargain, he, and his wife too, took an extra drop in their e'en, and their son Bernt had a taste of it too.

After that they sailed off homewards in their new boat. There was no other ballast in the boat but himself, his old woman, the children, and the Christmas provisions. His son Bernt sat by the mainsheet; his wife, helped by her next eldest son, held the sail ropes; Elias himself sat at the rudder, while the two younger brothers of twelve and four-teen were to take it in turns to bail out.

They had eight miles of sea to sail over, and when they got into the open, it was plain that the boat would be tested pretty stiffly on its first voyage. A gale was gradu-ally blowing up, and crests of foam began to break upon the heavy sea.

And now Elias saw what sort of boat he really had. She skipped over the waves like a sea mew; not so much as a splash came into the boat, and he therefore calculated that he would have no need to take in all his clews[7] against the wind, which an ordinary *femböring* would have been forced to do in such weather.

Out on the sea, not very far away from him, he saw another *femböring*, with a full crew and four clews in the sail, just like his own. It lay on the same course, and he thought it rather odd that he had not noticed it before. It made as if it would race him, and when Elias perceived

---

7. *clews*: The Klör, or clews, were rings in the corner of the sail to fasten it down by in a strong wind. *Setja ei Klo* = "take in the sail a clew." *Setja tvo* or *tri Klor* = "take in two or three clews," i.e., dimin-ish it still further as the wind grew stronger.

that, he could not for the life of him help letting out a clew again.

And now he went racing along like a dart, past capes and islands and rocks, till it seemed to Elias as if he had never had such a splendid sail before. Now, too, the boat showed itself what it really was, the best boat in Ranen.

The weather, meantime, had become worse, and they had already got a couple of dangerous seas right upon them. They broke in over the mainsheet in the forepart of the boat where Bernt sat, and sailed out again to leeward near the stern.

Since the gloom had deepened, the other boat had kept almost alongside, and they were now so close together that they could easily have pitched the bailing can from one to the other.

So they raced on, side by side, in constantly stiffer seas, till nightfall and beyond it. The fourth clew ought now to have been taken in again, but Elias didn't want to give in, and thought he might bide a bit till they took it in the other boat also, which they needs *must* do soon. Ever and anon the brandy flask was brought out and passed round, for they had now both cold and wet to hold out against.

The sea fire, which played on the dark billows near Elias's own boat, shone with an odd vividness in the foam round the other boat, just as if a fire shovel was plowing up and turning over the water. In the bright phosphorescence, he could plainly make out the rope ends on board her. He also could see distinctly the folks on board with their sou'westers on their heads, but as their larboard side lay nearest, of course, they all had their backs toward him, and were well-nigh hidden by the high-heeling hull.

Suddenly a tremendous roller burst upon them. Elias had long caught a glimpse of its white crest through the darkness, right over the prow where Bernt sat. It filled the whole boat for a moment; the planks shook and trembled beneath the weight of it, and then, as the boat, which had lain half on her beam ends, righted herself and sped on again, it streamed off behind to leeward.

While it was still upon him, he fancied he heard a hideous yell from the other boat, but when it was over, his wife, who sat by the shrouds, said with a voice which pierced his very soul: "Good God, Elias! The sea has carried off Martha and Nils!" Their two youngest children, nine, and seven years old, had been sitting in the hold near Bernt. Elias merely answered: "Don't let go the lines, Karen, or you'll lose yet more!"

They now had to take in the fourth clew, and,when this was done, Elias found that it would be well to take in the fifth and last clew too, for the gale was ever on the increase; but, on the other hand, in order to keep the boat free of the constantly heavier seas, he dare not lessen the sail a bit more than he was absolutely obliged to do, but they found that the scrap of sail they could carry gradually grew less and less. The sea seethed so that it drove right into their faces, and Bernt and his next eldest brother Anthony, who had hitherto helped his mother with the sail lines, had, at last, to hold in the yards, an expedient one only resorts to when the boat cannot bear even the last clew—here the fifth.

The companion boat, which had disappeared in the meantime, now suddenly ducked up alongside again with precisely the same amount of sail as Elias's boat, but he now began to feel that he didn't quite like the look of the crew on board there. The two who stood and held in the yards (he caught a glimpse of their pale faces beneath their sou'westers) seemed to him, by the odd light of the shining foam, more like corpses than men, nor did they speak a single word.

A little way off to larboard he again caught sight of the

high white back of a fresh roller coming through the dark, and he got ready betimes to receive it. The boat was laid to with its prow turned aslant towards the onrushing wave while the sail was made as large as possible so as to get up speed enough to cleave the heavy sea and sail out of it again. In rushed the roller with a roar like a chasm; again, for an instant, they lay on their beam ends, but, when it was over, the wife no longer sat by the sail ropes, nor did Anthony stand there any longer holding the yards —they had both gone overboard.

This time Elias fancied he heard the same hideous yell in the air, but in the midst of it he plainly heard his wife anxiously calling him by name. All that he said when he grasped the fact that she was washed overboard, was, "In Jesus' name!" His first and dearest wish was to follow after her, but he felt at the same time that it became him to save the rest of the freight he had on board, that is to say, Bernt and his other two sons, one twelve, the other fourteen years old, who had been baling out for a time, but had afterwards taken their places in the stern behind him.

Bernt had now to look to the yards all alone, and the other two helped as best they could. The rudder Elias durst not let slip, and he held it fast with a hand of iron, which continuous exertion had long since made insensible to feeling.

A moment afterwards the comrade boat ducked up again; it had vanished for an instant as before. Now, too, he saw more of the heavy man who sat in the stern there in the same place as himself. Out of his back, just below his sou'wester (as he turned round, it showed quite plainly), projected an iron spike six inches long, which Elias had no difficulty in recognizing again. And now, as he calmly thought it all over, he was quite clear about two things: one was that it was the draug[8] itself which was

---

8. *Draug*: A demon peculiar to the north Norwegian coast. It rides the seas in a half-beast. Compare Icelandic *draugr*.

steering its half-boat close beside him, and leading him to destruction; the other was that it was written in heaven that he was to sail his last course that night. For he who sees the draug on the sea is a doomed man. He said nothing to the others, lest they should lose heart, but in secret he commended his soul to God.

During the last hour or so he had been forced out of his proper course by the storm; the air also had become dense with snow; and Elias knew that he must wait till dawn before land could be sighted. Meanwhile he sailed along much the same as before. Now and then the boys in the stern complained that they were freezing; but, in the plight they were in now, that couldn't be helped, and, besides, Elias had something else to think about. A terrible longing for vengeance had come over him, and, but for the necessity of saving the lives of his three lads, he would have tried by a sudden turn to sink the accursed boat which kept alongside of him the whole time as if to mock him; he now understood its evil errand only too well. If the *kvejtepig* could reach the draug before, a knife or a gaff might surely do the same thing now, and he felt that he would gladly have given his life for one good grip of the being who had so mercilessly torn from him his dearest in this world and would fain have still more.

At three or four o'clock in the morning, they saw coming upon them through the darkness a breaker of such height that at first Elias thought they must be quite close ashore near the surf swell. Nevertheless, he soon recognized it for what it really was—a huge billow. Then it seemed to him as if there was a laugh over in the other boat, and something said, "There goes thy boat, Elias!" He, foreseeing the calamity, now cried aloud "In Jesus' name!" and then bade his sons to hold on with all their might to the withy-bands by the rowlocks when the boat went under, and not to let go till it was above the water again.

He made the elder of them go forward to Bernt, and himself held the youngest close by his side, stroked him once or twice furtively down the cheeks, and made sure that he had a good grip. The boat, literally buried beneath the foaming roller, was lifted gradually up by the bows and then went under. When it rose again out of the water, with the keel in the air, Elias, Bernt, and the twelve-year-old Martin lay alongside, holding on by the withy-bands; but the third of the brothers was gone.

They had now, first of all, to get the shrouds on one side cut through, so that the mast might come to the surface alongside instead of disturbing the balance of the boat below; and then they must climb up on the swaying bottom of the boat and stave in the keyholes, to let out the air which kept the boat too high in the water, and so ease her. After great exertions they succeeded, and Elias, who had got up on the top first, now helped the other two up after him.

There they sat through the long dark winter night, clinging convulsively on by their hands and knees to the boat's bottom, which was drenched by the billows again and again.

After the lapse of a couple of hours died Martin, whom his father had held up the whole time as far as he was able, of sheer exhaustion, and glided down into the sea. They had tried to cry for help several times, but gave it up at last as a bad job.

Whilst they two thus sat all alone on the bottom of the boat, Elias said to Bernt that he now must believe that he too was about to be "along o' mother," but that he had a strong hope that Bernt, at any rate, would be saved, if he only held out like a man. Then he told him all about the *draug*, whom he had struck below the neck with the *kve-jtepig*, and how it had now revenged itself upon him, and certainly would not forbear till it was "quits" with him.

It was towards nine o'clock in the morning when the gray dawn began to appear. Then Elias gave to Bernt, who sat alongside him, his silver watch with the brass chain, which he had snapped in two in order to drag it from beneath his closely buttoned jacket. He held on for a little time longer, but as it got lighter, Bernt saw that his father's face was deadly pale, his hair too had parted here and there, as often happens when death is at hand, and his skin was chafed off his hands from holding on to the keel. The son understood now that his father was nearly at the last gasp, and tried, so far as the pitching and tossing would allow it, to hold him up; but when Elias marked it, he said, "Nay, look to thyself, Bernt, and hold on fast. I go to mother—in Jesus' name!" And with that he cast himself down headlong from the top of the boat.

Everyone who has sat on the keel of a boat long enough knows that when the sea has got its own, it grows much calmer, though not immediately. Bernt now found it easier to hold on, and still more of hope came to him with the brightening day. The storm abated, and, when it got quite light, it seemed to him that he knew where he was, and that it was outside his own homestead, Kvalholm, that he lay driving.

He now began again to cry for help, but his chief hope was in a current which he knew bore landwards at a place where a headland broke in upon the surge, and there the water was calmer. And he did, in fact, drive closer and closer in, and came at last so near to one of the rocks that the mast, which was floating by the side of the boat all the time, surged up and down in the swell against the sloping cliff. Stiff as he now was in all his limbs from sitting and holding on, he nevertheless succeeded, after a great effort, in clambering up the cliff, where he hauled the mast ashore, and made the *femböring* fast.

The Finn girl, who was alone in the house, had been

thinking, for the last two hours, that she had heard cries for help from time to time, and as they kept on she mounted the hill to see what it was. There she saw Bernt up on the cliff, and the overturned *femböring* bobbing up and down against it. She immediately dashed down to the boat place, got out the old rowboat, and rowed along the shore and round the island right out to him.

Bernt lay sick under her care the whole winter through, and didn't go a fishing all that year. Ever after this, too, it seemed to folks as if the lad were a little bit daft.

On the open sea, he never would go again, for he had got the sea scare. He wedded the Finn girl, and moved over to the Malang, where he got him a clearing in the forest, and he lives there now, and is doing well, they say.

Jack of Sjöholm and the Gan-Finn

In the days of our forefathers, when there was nothing but wretched boats up in Nordland, and folks must needs buy fair winds by the sackful from the Gan[1]-Finn, it was not safe to tack about in the open sea in wintry weather. In those days a fisherman never grew old. It was mostly womenfolk and children, and the lame and halt, who were buried ashore.

Now there was once a boat's crew from Thjöttö in Helgeland, which had put to sea and worked its way right up to the East Lofotens.

But that winter the fish would not bite.

They lay to and waited week after week, till the month was out, and there was nothing for it but to turn home again with their fishing gear and empty boats.

But Jack of Sjöholm, who was with them, only laughed aloud, and said that if there were no fish there, fish would certainly be found higher northwards. Surely they hadn't rowed out all this distance only to eat up all their victuals, said he.

He was quite a young chap, who had never been out fishing before. But there was some sense in what he said for all that, thought the head fisherman.

And so they set their sails northwards.

On the next fishing ground, they fared no better than before, but they toiled away so long as their food held out.

And now they all insisted on giving it up and turning back.

---

1. *Gan*: This untranslatable word is a derivative of the Icelandic *Gandr*, and means magic of the black or malefic sort.

"If there's none here, there's sure to be some still higher up towards the north," opined Jack, "and if they had gone so far, they might surely go a little further still," quoth he.

So they tempted fortune from fishing ground to fishing ground, till they had ventured right up to Finmark[2]. But there a storm met them, and, try as they might to find shelter under the headlands, they were obliged at last to put out into the open sea again.

There they fared worse than ever. They had a hard time of it. Again and again the prow of the boat went under the heavy rollers, instead of over them, and later on in the day the boat foundered.

There they all sat helplessly on the keel in the midst of the raging sea, and they all complained bitterly against that fellow Jack, who had tempted them on, and led them into destruction. What would now become of their wives and children? They would starve now that they had none to care for them.

When it grew dark, their hands began to stiffen, and they were carried off by the sea, one by one.

And Jack heard and saw everything, down to the last shriek and the last clutch, and to the very end, they never ceased reproaching him for bringing them into such misery, and bewailing their sad lot.

"I must hold on tight now," said Jack to himself, for he was better even where he was than in the sea.

And so he tightened his knees on the keel, and held on fast till he had no feeling left in either hand or foot.

In the coal-black gusty night, he fancied he heard yells from one or other of the remaining boats' crews.

"They, too, have wives and children," thought he. "I wonder whether they have also a Jack to lay the blame upon!"

---

2. *Finmark*: The northernmost province of Norway, right within the Arctic circle.

Now while he thus lay there and drifted and drifted, and it seemed to him to be drawing towards dawn, he suddenly felt that the boat was in the grip of a strong shoreward current, and, sure enough, Jack got at last ashore. But whichever way he looked, he saw nothing but black sea and white snow.

Now as he stood there, speering and spying about him, he saw, far away, the smoke of a Finn gamme[3], which stood beneath a cliff, and he managed to scramble right up to it.

The Finn was so old that he could scarcely move. He was sitting in the midst of the warm ashes, and mumbling into a big sack, and neither spoke nor answered. Large yellow bumble-bees were humming about all over the snow, as if it were midsummer, and there was only a young lass there to keep the fire alight and give the old man his food. His grandsons and granddaughters were with the reindeer, far far away on the fjeld.

Here Jack got his clothes well-dried, and the rest he so much wanted. The Finn girl, Seimke, couldn't make too much of him; she fed him with reindeer milk and marrow-bones, and he lay down to sleep on silver fox skins.

Cozy and comfortable it was in the smoke there. But as he thus lay there, 'twixt sleep and wake, it seemed to him as if many odd things were going on round about him.

There stood the Finn in the doorway talking to his reindeer, although they were far away in the mountains. He barred the wolf's way, and threatened the bear with spells, and then he opened his skin sack, so that the storm howled and piped, and there was a swirl of ashes into the hut. And when all grew quiet again, the air was thick with yellow bumble-bees, which settled inside his furs, whilst he gabbled and mumbled and wagged his skull-like head.

But Jack had something else to think about besides marveling at the old Finn. No sooner did the heaviness of

3. *Finn gamme*: The huts peculiar to the Norwegian Finns.

slumber quit his eyes than he strolled down to his boat.

There it lay stuck fast on the beach and tilted right over like a trough, while the sea rubbed and rippled against its keel. He drew it far enough ashore to be beyond the reach of the sea wash.

But the longer he walked around and examined it, the more it seemed to him as if folks built boats rather for the sake of letting the sea in than for the sake of keeping the sea out. The prow was little better than a hog's snout for burrowing under the water, and the planking by the keel-piece was as flat as the bottom of a chest. Everything, he thought, must be arranged very differently if boats were to be really seaworthy. The prow must be raised one or two planks higher, at the very least, and made both sharp and supple, so as to bend before and cut through the waves at the same time, and then a fellow would have a chance of steering a boat smartly.

He thought of this day and night. The only relaxation he had was a chat with the Finn girl of an evening.

He couldn't help remarking that this Seimke had fallen in love with him. She strolled after him wherever he went, and her eyes always became so mournful when he went down towards the sea; she understood well enough that all his thoughts were bent upon going away.

And the Finn sat and mumbled among the ashes till his fur jacket regularly steamed and smoked.

But Seimke coaxed and wheedled Jack with her brown eyes, and gave him honeyed words as fast as her tongue could wag, till she drew him right into the smoke where the old Finn couldn't hear them.

The Gan-Finn turned his head right around.

"My eyes are stupid, and the smoke makes 'em run," said he. "What has Jack got hold of there?"

"Say it is the white ptarmigan you caught in the snare," whispered she.

24

Then she told him so softly that he thought it was his own thoughts speaking to him, that the Finn was angry and muttering mischief, and *jöjking*[4], against the boat which Jack wanted to build. If Jack were to complete it, she said, the Gan-Finn would no longer have any sale for his fair-winds in all Nordland. And then she warned him to look to himself and never get between the Finn and the gan-flies.

Then Jack felt that his boat might be the undoing of him. But the worse things looked, the more he tried to make the best of them.

In the gray dawn, before the Finn was up, he made his way towards the seashore.

But there was something very odd about the snow hills. They were so many and so long that there was really no end to them, and he kept on trampling in deep and deeper snow and never got to the seashore at all. Never before had he seen the northern lights last so long into the day. They blazed and sparkled, and long tongues of fire licked and hissed after him. He was unable to find either the beach or the boat, nor had he the least idea in the world where he really was.

At last he discovered that he had gone quite astray inland instead of down to the sea. But now, when he turned round, the sea fog came close up against him, so dense and gray that he could see neither hand nor foot before him.

By the evening he was well-nigh worn out with weariness, and was at his wits' end what to do.

Night fell, and the snowdrifts increased.

As now he sat him down on a stone and fell to brooding and pondering how he should escape with his life, a pair of snowshoes came gliding so smoothly towards him out of the sea fog and stood still just in front of his feet.

4. *Jöjking*: To sing songs (here magic songs), as the Finns do. Possibly derived from the Finnish verb *joikuu*, which means monotonous chanting.

"As you have found me, you may as well find the way back also," said he.

So he put them on, and let the snowshoes go their own way over hillside and steep cliff. He let not his own eyes guide him or his own feet carry him, and the swifter he went the denser the snowflakes and the driving sea spray came up against him, and the blast very nearly blew him off the snowshoes.

Up hill and down dale, he went over all the places where he had fared during the daytime, and it sometimes seemed as if he had nothing solid beneath him at all, but was flying in the air.

Suddenly the snowshoes stood stock still, and he was standing just outside the entrance of the Gan-Finn's hut.

There stood Seimke. She was looking for him.

"I sent my snowshoes after thee," said she, "for I marked that the Finn had bewitched the land so that thou shouldst not find the boat. Thy *life* is safe, for he has given thee shelter in his house, but it is not well for thee to see him this evening."

Then she smuggled him in, so that the Finn did not perceive it in the thick smoke, and she gave him meat and a place to rest upon.

But when he awoke in the night, he heard an odd sound, and there was a buzzing and a singing far away in the air:

> *"The Finn the boat can never bind,*
> *The Fly the boatman cannot find, but*
> *Round in aimless whirls doth wind."*

The Finn was sitting among the ashes and *jöjking*, and muttering till the ground quite shook, while Seimke lay with her forehead to the floor and her hands clasped tightly round the back of her neck, praying against him to the Finn god. Then Jack understood that the Gan-Finn was still seeking after him amidst the snowflakes and sea fog, and that his life was in danger from magic spells.

So he dressed himself before it was light, went out and came tramping in again all covered with snow, and said he had been after bears in their winter retreats. But never had he been in such a sea fog before; he had groped about far and wide before he found his way back into the hut again, though he stood just outside it.

The Finn sat there with his skin-wrappings as full of yellow flies as a beehive. He had sent them out searching in every direction, but back they had all come, and were humming and buzzing about him.

When he saw Jack in the doorway, and perceived that the flies had pointed truly, he grew somewhat milder, and laughed till he regularly shook within his skin-wrappings, and mumbled, "The bear we'll bind fast beneath the scullery sink, and his eyes I've turned all awry, so that he can't see his boat[5], and I'll stick a sleeping-peg in front of him till springtime."

But the same day, the Finn stood in the doorway and was busy making magic signs and strange strokes in the air.

Then he sent forth two hideous gan-flies, which flitted off on their errands, and scorched black patches beneath them in the snow wherever they went. They were to bring pain and sickness to a cottage down in the swamps, and spread abroad the Finn disease, which was to strike down a young bride at Bodö with consumption.

But Jack thought of nothing else night and day but how he could get the better of the Gan-Finn.

The lass Seimke wheedled him and wept and begged him, as he valued his life, not to try to get down to his boat again. At last, however, she saw it was no use—he had

---

5. I.e., the boat he (Jack) wanted to build.

made up his mind to be off.

Then she kissed his hands and wept bitterly. At least he must promise to wait till the Gan-Finn had gone right away to Jokmok[6] in Sweden.

On the day of his departure, the Finn went all round his hut with a torch and took stock.

Far away as they were, there stood the mountain pastures, with the reindeer and the dogs, and the Finn's people all drew near. The Finn took a tally of the beasts, and bade his grandsons not to let the reindeer stray too far while he was away, and could not guard them from wolves and bears. Then he took a sleeping potion and began to dance, turning round till his breath quite failed him, and he sank moaning to the ground. His furs were all that remained of him. His spirit had gone—gone all the way to Jokmok.

There the magicians were all sitting together in the dark sea fog beneath the shelter of the high mountain, and whispering about all manner of secret and hidden things, and blowing spirits into the novices of the black art.

But the gan-flies, humming and buzzing, went round and round the empty furs of the Gan-Finn like a yellow ring and kept watch.

In the night Jack was awakened by something pulling and tugging at him as if from far away. There was, as it were, a current of air and something threatened and called to him from the midst of the snowflakes outside—

"Until thou canst swim like the duck or the drake,
The egg[7] thou'dst be hatching no progress shall make;
The Finn shall ne'er let thee go southwards with sail,
For he'll screw off the wind and imprison the gale."

6. *Jokmok*: A mountain between Sweden and Norway.
7. I.e., the boat he would be building.

28

At the end of it the Gan-Finn was standing there, and bending right over him. The skin of his face hung down long and loose, and full of wrinkles, like an old reindeer skin, and there was a dizzying smoke in his eyes. Then Jack began to shiver and stiffen in all his limbs, and he knew that the Finn was bent upon bewitching him.

Then he set his face rigidly against it, so that the magic spells should not get at him, and thus they struggled with one another till the Gan-Finn grew green in the face, and was very near choking.

After that the sorcerers of Jokmok sent magic shots after Jack, and clouded his wits. He felt so odd, and whenever he was busy with his boat, and had put something to rights with it, something else would immediately go wrong, till at last he felt as if his head were full of pins and needles.

Then deep sorrow fell upon him. Try as he would, he couldn't put his boat together as he would have it, and it looked very much as if he would never be able to cross the sea again.

But in the summertime, Jack and Seimke sat together on the headland in the warm evenings, and the gnats buzzed and the fishes spouted close ashore in the stillness, and the eider duck swam about.

"If only someone would build me a boat as swift and nimble as a fish, and able to ride upon the billows like a sea mew!" sighed and lamented Jack, "then I could be off."

"Would you like me to guide you to Thjöttö?" said a voice up from the seashore.

There stood a fellow in a flat turned-down skin cap, whose face they couldn't see.

And right outside the boulders there, just where they had seen the eider duck, lay a long and narrow boat with high prow and stern, and the tar-boards were mirrored plainly in the clear water below; there was not so much as

29

a single knot in the wood.

"I would be thankful for any such guidance," said Jack.

When Seimke heard this, she began to cry and take on terribly. She fell upon his neck, and wouldn't let go, and raved and shrieked. She promised him her snowshoes, which would carry him through everything, and said she would steal for him the bone-stick from the Gan-Finn, so that he might find all the old lucky dollars that ever were buried, and would teach him how to make salmon-catching knots in the fishing lines, and how to entice the reindeer from afar. He should become as rich as the Gan-Finn, if only he wouldn't forsake her.

But Jack had only eyes for the boat down there. Then she sprang up, and tore down her black locks, and bound them round his feet, so that he had to wrench them off before he could get quit of her.

"If I stay here and play with you and the young reindeer, many a poor fellow will have to cling with broken nails to the keel of a boat,"[8] said he. "If you like to make it up, give me a kiss and a parting hug, or shall I go without them?"

Then she threw herself into his arms like a young wild cat, and looked straight into his eyes through her tears, and shivered and laughed, and was quite beside herself.

But when she saw she could do nothing with him, she rushed away, and waved her hands above her head in the direction of the gamme.

Then Jack understood that she was going to take counsel of the Gan-Finn, and that he had better take refuge in his boat before the way was closed to him. And, in fact, the boat had come so close up to the boulders, that he had only to step down upon the thwarts. The rudder glided into his hand, and aslant behind the mast sat someone at the prow, who hoisted and stretched the sail, but his face Jack

8. Meaning that he would never have a chance of building the new sort of boat that his mind was bent on.

30

could not see.

Away they went.

And such a boat for running before the wind Jack had never seen before. The sea stood up round about them like a deep snowdrift, although it was almost calm. But they hadn't gone very far before a nasty piping began in the air. The birds shrieked and made for land, and the sea rose like a black wall behind them.

It was the Gan-Finn who had opened his windsack, and sent a storm after them.

"One needs a full sail in the Finn-cauldron here," said something from behind the mast.

The fellow who had the boat in hand took such little heed of the weather that he did not so much as take in a single clew.

Then the Gan-Finn sent double knots[9] after them. They sped along in a wild dance right over the firth, and the sea whirled up in white columns of foam, reaching to the very clouds.

Unless the boat could fly as quick and quicker than a bird, it was lost.

Then a hideous laugh was heard to larboard—

> *"Anfinn Ganfinn gives mouth,*
> *And blows us right south;*
> *There's a crack[10] in the sack,*
> *With three clews we must tack."*

And heeling right over, with three clews in the sail, and the heavy foremost fellow astride on the sheer-strake with his huge sea boots dangling in the sea foam, away they scudded through the blinding spray right into the open sea, amidst the howling and roaring of the wind.

9. *Tvinde Knuder*: When the Finn tied *one* magic knot, he raised a gale, so two knots would give a tempest.
10. I.e., where the Gan-Finn let out the wind.

The billowy walls were so vast and heavy that Jack couldn't even see the light of day across the yards, nor could he exactly make out whether they were going under or over the sea trough.

The boat shook the sea aside as lightly and easily as if its prow were the slippery fin of a fish, and its planking was as smooth and fine as the shell of a tern's egg, but, look as he would, Jack couldn't see where these planks ended; it was just as if there was only half a boat and no more; and at last it seemed to him as if the whole of the front part came off in the sea foam, and they were scudding along under sail in half a boat.

When night fell, they went through the sea fire, which glowed like hot embers, and there was a prolonged and hideous howling up in the air to windward.

And cries of distress and howls of mortal agony answered the wind from all the upturned boat keels they sped by, and many hideously pale-looking folks clutched hold of their thwarts. The gleam of the sea fire cast a blue glare on their faces, and they sat, and gaped, and glared, and yelled at the blast.

Suddenly he awoke, and something cried, "Now thou art at home at Thjöttö, Jack!"

And when he had come to himself a bit, he recognized where he was. He was lying over against the boulders near his boathouse at home. The tide had come so far inland that a border of foam gleamed right up in the potato field, and he could scarcely keep his feet for the blast. He sat down in the boathouse, and began scratching and marking out the shape of the draugboat in the black darkness till sleep overtook him.

When it was light in the morning, his sister came down to him with a basket of meat. She didn't greet him as if he were a stranger, but behaved as if it were the usual thing for her to come thus every morning. But when he began telling her all about his voyage to Finmark, and the Gan-Finn, and the draugboat he had come home in at night, he perceived that she only grinned and let him chatter. And all that day he talked about it to his sister and his brothers and his mother, until he arrived at the conclusion that they thought him a little out of his wits. When he mentioned the draugboat, they smiled amongst themselves, and evidently went out of their way to humor him. But they might believe what they liked, if only he could carry out what he wanted to do and be left to himself in the out-of-the-way old boathouse.

"One should go with the stream," thought Jack, and if they thought him crazy and out of his wits, he ought to behave so that they might beware of interfering with him and disturbing him in his work.

So he took a bed of skins with him down to the boathouse, and slept there at night, but in the daytime he perched himself on a pole on the roof, and bellowed out that now he was sailing. Sometimes he rode astraddle the roof ridge, and dug his sheath knife deep into the rafters, so that people might think he fancied himself at sea, holding fast onto the keel of a boat.

Whenever folks passed by, he stood in the doorway and turned up the whites of his eyes so hideously, that everyone who saw him was quite scared. As for the people at home, it was as much as they dared to stick his meat-basket into the boathouse for him. So they sent it to him by his youngest sister, merry little Malfri, who would sit and talk with him, and thought it such fun when he made toys and playthings for her, and talked about the boat which should go like a bird, and sail as no other boat had ever sailed.

If anyone chanced to come upon him unexpectedly, and tried to peep and see what he was about in the boathouse there, he would creep up into the timber-loft and bang and pitch the boards and planks about, so that they didn't know exactly where to find him, and were glad enough to be off. But one and all made haste to climb over the hill again when they heard him fling himself down at full length and send peal after peal of laughter after them.

So that was how Jack got folks to leave him at peace.

He worked best at night when the storm tore and tugged at the stones and birch-bark of the turf roof, and the sea wrack came right up to the boathouse door.

When it piped and whined through the fissured walls, and the fine snowflakes flitted through the cracks, the model of the draugboat stood plainest before him. The winter days were short, and the wick of the train-oil lamp, which hung over him as he worked, cast deep shadows, so that the darkness came soon and lasted a long way into the morning, when he sought sleep in his bed of skins with a heap of shavings for his pillow.

He spared no pains or trouble. If there were a board which would not run into the right groove with the others, though ever so little, he would take out a whole row of them and plane them all round again and again.

Now, one night just before Christmas, he had finished all but the uppermost planking and the gabs. He was working so hard to finish up that he took no count of time.

The plane was sending the shavings flying their briskest when he came to a dead stop at something black which was moving along the plank.

It was a large and hideous fly which was crawling about and feeling and poking all the planks in the boat. When it reached the lowest keelboard, it whirred with its wings and buzzed. Then it rose and swept above it in the air till, all at once, it swerved away into the darkness.

Jack's heart sank within him. Such doubt and anguish came upon him. He knew well enough that no good errand had brought the gan-fly buzzing over the boat like that.

34

So he took the train-oil lamp and a wooden club, and began to test the prow and light up the boarding and thump it well, and go over the planks one by one. And in this way, he went over every bit of the boat from stem to stern, both above and below. There was not a nail or a rivet that he really believed in now.

But now neither the shape nor the proportions of the boat pleased him anymore. The prow was too big, and the whole cut of the boat all the way down the gunwale had something of a twist and a bend and a swerve about it, so that it looked like the halves of two different boats put together, and the half in front didn't fit with the half behind. As he was about to look into the matter still further (and he felt the cold sweat bursting out of the roots of his hair), the train-oil lamp went out and left him in blank darkness.

Then he could contain himself no longer. He lifted his club and burst open the boathouse door, and, snatching up a big cowbell, he began to swing it about him and ring and ring with it through the black night.

"Art thou chiming for me, Jack?" something asked. There was a sound behind him like the surf sucking at the shore, and a cold blast blew into the boathouse.

There on the keel-stick sat someone in a sloppy gray sea-jacket, and with a print cap drawn down over its ears, so that its skull looked like a low tassel.

Jack gave a great start. This was the very being he had been thinking of in his wild rage. Then he took the large baling can and flung it at the draug.

But right through the draug it went, and rattled against the wall behind, and back again it came whizzing about Jack's ears, and if it had struck him he would never have gotten up again.

The old fellow, however, only blinked his eyes a little savagely.

"Fie!" cried Jack, and spat at the uncanny thing—and back into his face again he got as good as he gave.

"There you have your wet clout back again!" cried a laughing voice.

But the same instant Jack's eyes were opened, and he saw a whole boat-building establishment on the seashore.

And, there, ready and rigged out on the bright water, lay an *ottring*[11], so long and shapely and shining that his eyes could not feast on it enough.

The old 'un blinked with satisfaction. His eyes became more and more glowing.

"If I could guide you back to Helgeland," said he, "I could put you in the way of gaining your bread too. But you must pay me a little tax for it. In every seventh boat you build, 'tis *I* who must put in the keelboard."

Jack felt as if he were choking. He felt that the boat was dragging him into the very jaws of an abomination.

"Or do you fancy you'll worm the trick out of me for nothing?" said the gaping grinning draug.

Then there was a whirring sound, as if something heavy was hovering about the boathouse, and there was a laugh: "If you want the *seaman's* boat you must take the *dead man's* boat along with it. If you knock three times tonight on the keel-piece with the club, you shall have such help in building boats that the like of them will not be found in all Nordland."

Twice did Jack raise his club that night, and twice he laid it aside again.

But the *ottring* lay and frisked and sported in the sea before his eyes, just as he had seen it, all bright and new with fresh tar, and with the ropes and fishing gear just put in. He kicked and shook the fine slim boat with his foot just to see how light and high she could rise on the waves above the water line.

11. *Ottring*: An eight-oared boat.

And once, twice, thrice, the club smote against the keel-piece.

So that was how the first boat was built at Sjöholm.

Thick as birds together stood a countless number of people on the headland in the autumn, watching Jack and his brothers putting out in the new *ottring*.

It glided through the strong current so that the foam was like a trench all round it.

Now it was gone, and now it ducked up again like a sea mew, and past skerries and capes it whizzed like a dart.

Out in the fishing grounds the folks rested upon their oars and gaped. Such a boat they had never seen before.

But if in the first year it was an *ottring*, next year it was a broad heavy *femböring* for winter fishing which made the folks open their eyes.

And every boat that Jack turned out was lighter to row and swifter to sail than the one before it.

But the largest and finest of all was the last that stood on the stocks on the shore.

This was the *seventh*.

Jack walked to and fro, and thought about it a good deal, but when he came down to see it in the morning, it seemed to him, oddly enough, to have grown in the night and, what is more, was such a wondrous beauty that he was struck dumb with astonishment. There it lay ready at last, and folks were never tired of talking about it.

Now, the bailiff who ruled over all Helgeland in those days was an unjust man who laid heavy taxes upon the people, taking double weight and tally both of fish and of eiderdown, nor was he less grasping with the tithes and grain dues. Wherever his fellows came, they fleeced and flayed. No sooner, then, did the rumor of the new boats reach him than he sent his people out to see what truth was in it, for he himself used to go fishing in the fishing grounds with large crews. When thus his fellows came

37

back and told him what they had seen, the bailiff was so taken with it that he drove straightway over to Sjöholm, and one fine day down he came swooping on Jack like a hawk. "Neither tithe nor tax hast thou paid for thy livelihood, so now thou shalt be fined as many half-marks of silver as thou hast made boats," said he.

Ever louder and fiercer grew his rage. Jack should be put in chains and irons and be transported northwards to the fortress of Skraar, and be kept so close that he should never see sun or moon more.

But when the bailiff had rowed round the *femböring*, and feasted his eyes upon it, and seen how smart and shapely it was, he agreed at last to let mercy go before justice, and was content to take the *femböring* in lieu of a fine.

Then Jack took off his cap and said that if there was one man more than another to whom he would like to give the boat, it was his honor the bailiff.

So off the magistrate sailed with it.

Jack's mother and sister and brothers cried bitterly at the loss of the beautiful *femböring*, but Jack stood on the roof of the boathouse and laughed fit to split.

And towards autumn the news spread that the bailiff with his eight men had gone down with the *femböring* in the West-fjord.

But in those days there was quite a changing about of boats all over Nordland, and Jack was unable to build a tenth part of the boats required of him. Folks from near and far hung about the walls of his boathouse, and it was quite a favor on his part to take orders, and agree to carry them out. A whole score of boats soon stood beneath the penthouse on the strand.

He no longer troubled his head about every *seventh* boat, or cared to know which it was or what befell it. If a boat foundered now and then, so many the more got off and did well, so that, on the whole, he made a very good thing indeed out of it. Besides, surely folks could pick and choose their own boats, and take which they liked best.

But Jack got so great and mighty that it was not advisable for anyone to thwart him, or interfere where he ruled and reigned.

Whole rows of silver dollars stood in the barrels in the loft, and his boat-building establishment stretched over all the islands of Sjöholm.

One Sunday his brothers and merry little Malfri had gone to church in the *femböring*. When evening came, and they hadn't come home, the boatman came in and said that someone had better sail out and look after them, as a gale was blowing up.

Jack was sitting with a plumb-line in his hand, taking the measurements of a new boat, which was to be bigger and statelier than any of the others, so that it was not well to disturb him.

"Do you fancy they've gone out in a rotten old tub, then?" bellowed he. And the boatman was driven out as quickly as he had come.

But at night Jack lay awake and listened. The wind whined outside and shook the walls, and there were cries from the sea far away. And just then there came a knocking at the door, and someone called him by name.

"Go back whence you came," cried he, and nestled more snugly in his bed.

Shortly afterwards there came the fumbling and the scratching of tiny fingers at the door.

"Can't you leave me at peace o' nights?" he bawled, "or must I build me another bedroom?"

But the knocking and the fumbling for the latch outside continued, and there was a sweeping sound at the door, as of someone who could not open it. And there was a stretching of hands towards the latch ever higher and higher.

But Jack only lay there and laughed. "The *fembörings* that are built at Sjöholm don't go down before the first blast that blows," mocked he.

Then the latch chopped and hopped till the door flew wide open, and in the doorway stood pretty Malfri and her mother and brothers. The sea fire shone about them, and they were dripping with water.

Their faces were pale and blue, and pinched about the corners of the mouth, as if they had just gone through their death agony. Malfri had one stiff arm round her mother's neck; it was all torn and bleeding, just as when she had gripped her for the last time. She railed and lamented, and begged back her young life from him.

So now he knew what had befallen them.

Out into the dark night and the darker weather he went straightway to search for them, with as many boats and folk as he could get together. They sailed and searched in every direction, and it was in vain.

But towards day the *femböring* came drifting homewards bottom upwards, and with a large hole in the keelboard.

Then he knew who had done the deed.

But since the night when the whole of Jack's family went down, things were very different at Sjöholm.

In the daytime, so long as the hammering and the banging and the planing and the clinching rang about his ears, things went along swimmingly, and the frames of boat after boat rose thick as sea fowl on an *æggevær*[12].

But no sooner was it quiet of an evening than he had company. His mother bustled and banged about the house, and opened and shut drawers and cupboard, and the stairs creaked with the heavy tread of his brothers going up to their bedrooms.

12. Æggevær: A place where sea-birds' eggs abound.

40

At night no sleep visited his eyes, and sure enough pretty Malfri came to his door and sighed and groaned.

Then he would lie awake there and think, and reckon up how many boats with false keelboards he might have sent to sea. And the longer he reckoned the more draugboats he made of it.

Then he would plump out of bed and creep through the dark night down to the boathouse. There he held a light beneath the boats, and banged and tested all the keelboards with a club to see if he couldn't hit upon the *seventh*. But he neither heard nor felt a single board give way. One was just like another. They were all hard and supple, and the wood, when he scraped off the tar, was white and fresh.

One night he was so tormented by an uneasiness about the new *sekstring*[13], which lay down by the bridge ready to set off next morning, that he had no peace till he went down and tested its keelboard with his club.

But while he sat in the boat, and was bending over the thwart with a light, there was a gulping sound out at sea, and then came such a vile stench of rottenness. The same instant he heard a wading sound, as of many people coming ashore, and then up over the headland he saw a boat's crew coming along.

They were all crooked-looking creatures, and they all leaned right forward and stretched out their arms before them. Whatever came in their way, both stone and stour[14], they went right through it, and there was neither sound nor shriek.

Behind them came another boat's crew, big and little, grown men and little children, rattling and creaking.

And crew after crew came ashore and took the path leading to the headland.

When the moon peeped forth, Jack could see right into

13. *Sekstring*: A contraction of *Sexæring*, i.e., a boat with six oars.
14. stour: English dialect word (the Norse is *staur*) meaning impediments of any kind.

41

their skeletons. Their faces glared, and their mouths gaped open with glistening teeth, as if they had been swallowing water. They came in heaps and shoals, one after the other; the place quite swarmed with them.

Then Jack perceived that here were all they whom he had tried to count and reckon up as he lay in bed, and a fit of fury came upon him.

He rose in the boat and spanked his leather breeches behind and cried: "You would have been even more than you are already if Jack hadn't built his boats!"

But now like an icy whizzing blast they all came down upon him, staring at him with their hollow eyes.

They gnashed their teeth, and each one of them sighed and groaned for his lost life.

Then Jack, in his horror, put out from Sjöholm.

But the sail slackened, and he glided into dead water[15]. There, in the midst of the still water, was a floating mass of rotten swollen planks. All of them had once been shaped and fashioned together, but were now burst and sprung, and slime and green mold and filth and nastiness hung abut them.

Dead hands grabbed at the corners of them with their white knuckles and couldn't grip fast. They stretched themselves across the water and sank again.

Then Jack let out all his clews and sailed and sailed and tacked according as the wind blew.

He glared back at the rubbish behind him to see if those *things* were after him. Down in the sea all the dead hands were writhing, and tried to strike him with gaffs astern.

Then there came a gust of wind whining and howling, and the boat drove along betwixt white seething rollers.

The weather darkened, thick snowflakes filled the air, and the rubbish around him grew greener.

15. Dead water: *Daudvatn* (Dan. *Dödvand*), water in which there is no motion.

In the daytime he took the cormorants far away in the gray mists for his landmarks, and at night they screeched about his ears.

And the birds flitted and flitted continually, but Jack sat still and looked out upon the hideous cormorants.

At last the sea fog lifted a little, and the air began to be alive with bright, black, buzzing flies. The sun burned, and far away inland the snowy plains blazed in its light.

He recognized very well the headland and shore where he was now able to lay to. The smoke came from the gamme up on the snow hill there. In the doorway sat the Gan-Finn. He was lifting his pointed cap up and down, up and down, by means of a thread of sinew, which went right through him, so that his skin creaked.

And up there also sure enough was Seimke.

She looked old and angular as she bent over the reindeer skin that she was spreading out in the sunny weather. But she peeped beneath her arm as quick and nimble as a cat with kittens, and the sun shone upon her, and lit up her face and pitch-black hair.

She leaped up so briskly, and shaded her eyes with her hand, and looked down at him. Her dog barked, but she quieted it so that the Gan-Finn should mark nothing.

Then a strange longing came over him, and he put ashore.

He stood beside her, and she threw her arms over her head, and laughed and shook and nestled close up to him, and cried and pleaded, and didn't know what to do with herself, and ducked down upon his bosom, and threw herself on his neck, and kissed and fondled him, and wouldn't let him go.

But the Gan-Finn had noticed that there was something amiss, and sat all the time in his furs, and mumbled and muttered to the gan-flies, so that Jack dare not get between him and the doorway.

The Finn was angry.

Since there had been such a changing about of boats over all Nordland, and there was no more sale for his fair winds, he was quite ruined, he complained He was now so poor that he would very soon have to go about and beg his bread. And of all his reindeer he had only a single doe left, who went about there by the house.

Then Seimke crept behind Jack and whispered to him to bid for this doe. Then she put the reindeer skin around her, and stood inside the gamme door in the smoke, so that the Gan-Finn only saw the gray skin, and fancied it was the reindeer they were bringing in.

Then Jack laid his hand upon Seimke's neck, and began to bid.

The pointed cap ducked and nodded, and the Finn spat in the warm air, but sell his reindeer he would not.

Jack raised his price.

But the Finn heaved up the ashes all about him, and threatened and shrieked. The flies came as thick as snowflakes; the Finn's furry wrappings were alive with them.

Jack bid and bid till it reached a whole bushel load of silver, and the Finn was ready to jump out of his skins.

Then he stuck his head under his furs again, and mumbled and *jöjked* till the amount rose to seven bushels of silver.

Then the Gan-Finn laughed till he nearly split. He thought the reindeer would cost the purchaser a pretty penny.

But Jack lifted Seimke up, and sprang down with her to his boat, and held the reindeer skin behind him, against the Gan-Finn.

And they put off from land, and went to sea.

Seimke was so happy, and smote her hands together, and took her turn at the oars.

44

The northern light shot out like a comb, all greeny-red and fiery, and licked and played upon her face. She talked to it, and fought it with her hands, and her eyes sparkled. She used both tongue and mouth and rapid gestures as she exchanged words with it.

Then it grew dark, and she lay on his bosom, so that he could feel her warm breath. Her black hair lay right over him, and she was as soft and warm to touch as a ptarmigan when it is frightened and its blood throbs.

Jack put the reindeer skin over Seimke, and the boat rocked them to and fro on the heavy sea as if it were a cradle.

They sailed on and on till nightfall; they sailed on and on till they saw neither headland nor island nor sea bird in the outer skerries more.

Tug of War

For the last two or three days the weather had been terrific, but on the third day it so far cleared up that one of the men who belonged to the fishing station thought that they might manage to drag the nets a bit that day. The others, however, were not inclined to venture out. Now it is the custom for the various crews to lend each other a hand in pushing off the boats, and so it happened now. When, however, they came to the *femböring*, which was drawn up a good distance ashore, they found the oars and the thwarts turned upside down in the boat, and, more than that, despite all their exertions, it was impossible to move the boat from the spot. They tried once, twice, thrice, but it was of no use. But then one of them, who was known to have second sight, said that, from what he saw, it would be best not to touch the boat at all that day; it was too heavy for the might of man to move. One of the crew, however, who belonged to the fishing station (he was a smart lad of fourteen), was amusing them all the time with all manner of pranks and tomfoolery. He now caught up a heavy stone and pitched it with all his might right into the stern of the boat. Then, suddenly and plainly visible to them all, out of the boat rushed a draug in seaman's clothes, but with a heavy crop of seaweed instead of a head. It had been weighing down the boat by sitting in the stern, and now dashed into the sea, so that the foam spurted all over them. After that the *femböring* glided quite smoothly into the water. Then the man, with second sight, looked at the boy, and said that he should not have done so. But the lad went on laughing as before, and said he didn't believe in such stuff. When they had come home in the evening, and the folks lay sleeping in the fishing station, they heard, about twelve o'clock at night, the lad yelling for help; it even seemed to one of them, by the light of the train-oil lamp, as if a heavy hand were stretching forward from the door right up to the bench on which the lad lay. The lad, yelling and struggling, had already been dragged as far as the door before the others had so far come to their senses as to think of grasping him round the body to prevent him from being dragged right out. And now, in mid-doorway, a hard fight began, the draug dragging him by the legs while the whole crew tugged against him with the boy's arms and upper limbs. Thus, amidst yelling and groaning, they swayed to and fro all through the midnight hour, backwards and forwards, in the half-open door, and now the draug, and now the men, had the most of the boy on their side of the doorway. All at once the draug let go, so that the whole crew fell higgledy-piggledy backwards onto the floor. Then they found that the boy was dead; it was only then that the draug had let him go.

"The Earth Draws"

There was once a young salesman at the storekeeper's at Sörvaag.

He was fair, with curly hair, shrewd blue eyes, and so smart, and obliging, and handsome, that all the girls in the town got themselves sent on errands, and made pilgrimages to the shop on purpose to see him. Moreover, he was so smart and skillful in everything he put his hand to, that the storekeeper never would part with him.

Now it happened one day that he went out to a fishing station for his principal.

The current was dead against him, so he rode close in shore.

All at once he saw a little ring in the rocky wall a little above high-water mark. He thought it was the sort of ring which is used for fastening boats to, so he fancied it would not do any harm to rest a bit and lay to ashore, and have a snack of something, for he had been pulling at the oars from early morn.

But when he took hold of the ring to run his boatline through it, it fitted round his finger so tightly that he had to tug at it. He tugged, and out of the mountainside with a rush came a large drawer. It was brimful of silk neckerchiefs and women's frippery.

He was amazed, and began pondering the matter over.

Then he saw what looked like rusty flakes of iron in rows right over the whole mountainside, exactly resembling the slit of his own drawer.

He had now got the ring on his finger, and must needs try if it would open the other slits also. And out he drew drawer after drawer full of gold bracelets and silver bracelets, glass pearls, brooches and rings, bracelets and laced caps, yarn, nightcaps and woolen drawers, coffee, sugar, groats, tobacco pipes, buttons, hooks and eyes, knives, axes, and scythes.

He drew out drawer after drawer; there was no end to the display they made.

But all round about him he heard, as it were, the humming of a crowd and the tramp of sea boots. There was a hubbub, as if they were rolling hogsheads over a bridge and hoisting sails against the wind, and out from the sea, sounded the stroke of oars and the bumping of boats putting ashore.

Then he began to have an inkling that he had laid to his boat at a mooring-ring belonging to the underground folk, and had lit right upon their landing place where they deposited their wares.

He stood there looking into a drawer of meerschaum pipes. They were finer than any he had thought it possible to find in the whole world.

Then he felt, as it were, the blow of a heavy hand which tried to thrust him aside, but, at the same time, someone laughed so merrily close by. The same instant he saw a young woman in the fore part of his boat. She was leaning, with broad shoulders and hairy arms, over a meal sack. Her eyes laughed and shot forth sparks as from a smithy in the dark, but her face was oddly pale.

Then she vanished altogether like a vision.

He was glad when he got down into his boat again, and pushed off and rode away.

But when he got out into the sound, and slackened speed a bit, he perceived that the ring still sat upon his finger.

His first thought was to tear it off and fling it into the sea, but then it sat tighter than ever.

It was so curiously wrought and fretted and engraved

51

that he must needs examine it more curiously, and the longer he looked at it the stranger the gold whereof it was wrought gleamed and glistened. Turn it as he would to examine its spirals, he could never make out where they began and where they ended.

But as he sat there and looked and looked at it, the black crackling and sparkling eyes of that pale face stood out more and more plainly before his eyes. He didn't exactly know whether he thought her ugly or handsome—the uncanny creature!

The ring he now meant to keep, come what might.

And home he rowed, and said not a word to anybody of what had happened to him.

But from that day forth a strange restlessness came over him.

When he was sweeping out the shop or measuring goods, he would suddenly stand there in a brown study, and fancy he was right away at the landing-stage in the mountainside, and the black woman was laughing at him over the meal sack.

Out yonder he must needs venture once more, and put his ring to the test, though it cost him his life.

And in the course of the summer, his boat lay over at the mountainside in the self-same place as before.

When he had opened the drawer with his gold ring, he caught sight of the broad-shouldered woman. Her eyes sparkled, and had a wild look about them, and she peered curiously at him.

And, every time he came, he seemed to be more expected, and she was more and more gladsome. They became quite old acquaintances, and she was always waiting for him there.

But at home he grew gloomy and silent. Yet, although he bethought him that it was all sorcery, and her arms were hairy almost like a beast's, and although he determined and really tried to keep away, he still could not help going thither, and whenever he had been away from her a whole week, she grew quite unmanageable, and laughed and shrieked when she saw him coming again.

And he always heard the noise and the bustle of many people all about him, but never could he see anything. It seemed to him, however, as if they all lay a little way off and pulled their boat aside for him to pass. His boat, too, was always nicely baled out, and the oars and sails righted and trimmed. The cable, too, was fastened for him whenever he came, and thrown to him whenever he went away.

Now and then she so managed it that he caught a glimpse into their warehouses and their bright halls in the mountainside, and at such times she seemed to be enticing him after her. And then, on his way home, he would shudder. "What," thought he, "if the mountain wall were to shut behind me?" And every time he was right glad that he had been so far on his guard and had come off scot free.

And now, towards autumn, he grew more at his ease. He really made up his mind to try to give up these journeys. He set to work in real earnest, so that he had no time for thought, and plunged into his business with fiery impetuosity.

But when Christmastide drew nigh with its snowflakes and darkness, such strange fancies came over him.

Whenever he went into the dark drafty nooks and corners, he saw the strong, heavily-built shape before him. She laughed and called to him, and shrieked and sent him messages by the blast. And then a strong desire came upon him.

And one day he was unable to hold out any longer, so off he went.

He fancied he caught a glimpse of her a long way off. She was casting huge boulders aside so as to see and follow the course of the boat, and she beckoned and greeted him through the drizzle and the mist. It was as though the current was bearing him thither all the time.

When he came up, the sea seethed and boiled for the crowds that were in it, though he saw them not. They waded out to him and drew his boat ashore, and steps and a bridge lay there ready for his feet. But right at the top stood she, and her breath came heavily, and she leaned towards him and drew him with those bold eyes of hers set in that face as pale as night. She went swiftly inland, looked behind her, and beckoned him after her, and then she threw open the door of an old iron safe in the midst of the wall.

On its shelves sparkled a bridal crown and a shining girdle and breastplate and a kirtle and all manner of bridal finery.

There she stood, and her breath came straining hot and heavy through her white teeth, and she smiled and ogled him archly. He felt her take hold of him, and it was as though a darkness fell around him.

Then all at once, as if in a gleam of twilight, he saw the whole trading place, vast and wealthy and splendid, all round about him with its haven, warehouses, and trading ships. She stretched out her hands and pointed to it, as if she would say that he should be the lord and master of the whole of it.

A cold shiver ran through him; he perceived that it led right into the mountain.

And out he rushed.

He cut the cable through with his knife, and wrenched the ring from his finger, and cast it into the sea, and off he rowed, so that the sea was like a foaming gulf around him.

When he got home to his work again, and the bustle of the Christmas season began, he felt as if he had awakened from a heavy nightmare or an evil dream. He felt so light of heart. He chatted gaily with customers over the counter, and his old life went on much the same as before. And everything he put his hand to went along as smooth as butter.

But the tradesman's daughter stuck her head into the shop not just once or twice. She looked and smiled at him in shy admiration. Never had he remarked before what taking ways were hers, or noticed how bonnie and bright the lassie was, and how graceful and supple she looked as she stood in the doorway. And ever since the tradesman's daughter had looked so strangely at him, he had no thought for anyone but her. He was always thinking what a way she had of holding her head, and how slim she looked when she walked about, and what quick and lively blue eyes she had, just like merry twinkling stars.

He would lay awake o' nights, and reflect upon his grievous abominable sin in lowering himself to the level of an uncanny monster, and right glad was he that he had cast the ring away.

But on Christmas Eve, when the shop was shut and the house folks and servants were making ready for the festival in kitchen and parlor, the shopkeeper took him aside into his counting house. If he liked his daughter, said he, there was no impediment that he could see. Let him take heart and woo her, for it hadn't escaped him how she was moping about all lovesick on his account. He himself, said the shopkeeper, was old, and would like to retire from business.

The good-looking shopman did not wait to be asked twice. He wooed straightway, and, before the Christmas cheer was on the table, he got yes for an answer.

Then years and years passed over them, and they thrived and prospered in house and home.

They had pretty and clever children. He rejoiced in his wife; nothing was too good for her, and honor and ease were her portion, both at home and abroad.

But in the seventh year, when it was drawing towards Yuletide, such a strange restlessness came over him. He wandered about all by himself, and could find peace nowhere.

His wife fretted and sorrowed over it. She knew not what it could be, and it seemed to her that he oddly avoided her. He would wander for hours together about the dark packhouse loft, among coffers and casks and barrels and sacks, and it was as though he didn't like folks to come thither when he was there.

Now it chanced on the day before Little Christmas Eve[1] that one of the workpeople had to fetch something from the loft.

There stood the master, deep in thought, by one of the meal sacks, staring down on the ground before him.

"Don't you see the iron ring down in the floor there?" he asked.

But the man saw no ring.

"I see it there—the earth draws," he sighed heavily.

On Little Christmas Eve, he was nowhere to be found, nor on the day after, though they searched for him high and low, and made inquiries about him everywhere amidst the Yuletide bustle and merriment.

But late on Christmas Eve, while they were all running about in the utmost anxiety, not knowing whether they should lay the table or not, all at once, in he came through the door.

He longed so much for both meat and drink, he said, and he was so happy and merry and jovial the whole evening through, that they all clean forgot the fright they had been in.

For a whole year afterwards, he was chatty and sociable as before, and he made so much of his wife that it was quite absurd. He bore her in his hands, so to speak, and

1. *Lille Jule-aften*, i.e., the day before Christmas Eve (*Jule-aften*).

absolutely could not do enough for her.

But when it drew towards Yuletide again, and the darkest time of the year, the same sort of restlessness came over him. It was as though they only saw his shadow amongst them, and he went moping about the packhouse loft again, and lingering there.

On Little Christmas Eve the same thing happened as before—he disappeared.

His wife and the people of the house went about in a terrible way, and were filled with astonishment and alarm.

And on Christmas Eve he suddenly stepped into the room again, and was merry and jovial, as he generally was. But when the lights had burnt out, and they all had gone to bed, his wife could hold her tongue no longer; she burst into tears, and begged him to tell her where he had been.

Then he thrust her roughly from him, and his eyes shot sparks, as if he were downright crazy. He implored her, for their mutual happiness's sake, never to ask him such a question again.

Time went on, and the same thing happened every year.

When the days grew dark, he moped about by himself, all gloomy and silent, and seemed bent upon hiding himself away from people, and on Little Christmas Eve he always disappeared, though nobody ever saw him go. And punctually on Christmas Eve, at the very moment when they were about to lay the table, he all at once came in at the door, happy and contented with them all.

But just before every autumn, towards the dark days, always earlier than the year before, this restlessness came over him, and he moped about with it, moodier and shyer of people than ever.

His wife never questioned him, but a load of sorrow lay

upon her, and it seemed to her to grow heavier and more crushing, since she seemed no longer able to take care of him, and he no longer seemed to belong to her.

Now one year, when it was again drawing nigh to Yuletide, he began roaming about as usual, heavy and cast down, and the day before Little Christmas Eve he took his wife along with him into the packhouse loft.

"Do you see anything there by the meal sack?" he asked.

But she saw nothing.

Then he gripped her by the hand, and begged and implored her to remain, and go with him there at night. As his life was dear to him, said he, he would fain try and stay at home that day.

In the course of the night, he tightly grasped her hand time after time, and sighed and groaned. She felt that he was holding on to her, and striving hard, and with all his might, against *something*.

When morning came, it was all over. He was happier and lighter of mood than she had seen him for a long, long time, and he remained at home.

On that Christmas Eve there was such a hauling and carrying-on upstairs from both shop and cellar, and the candles shone till all the window panes sparkled again. It was the first real festival he had ever spent in his own house, he said, and he meant to make a regular banquet of it.

But when, as the custom was, the people of the house came in one by one, and drank to the healths of their master and mistress, he grew paler and paler and whiter and whiter, as if his blood were being sucked out of him and drained away.

"The earth draws!" he shrieked, and there was a look of horror in his eyes.

Immediately afterwards he sat there—dead!

"The Cormorants of Andvær"

Outside Andvær lies an island, the haunt of wild birds, which no man can land upon, be the sea never so quiet; the sea swell girds it round about with sucking whirlpools and dashing breakers.

On fine summer days, something sparkles there through the sea foam like a large gold ring, and, time out of mind, folks have fancied there was a treasure there left by some pirates of old.

At sunset, sometimes, there looms forth from thence a vessel with a castle astern, and a glimpse is caught now and then of an old-fashioned galley. There it lies as if in a tempest, and carves its way along through heavy white rollers.

Along the rocks sit the cormorants in a long black row, lying in wait for dogfish.

But there was a time when one knew the exact number of these birds. There was never more nor less of them than twelve, while upon a stone, out in the sea mist, sat the thirteenth, but it was only visible when it rose and flew right over the island.

The only persons who lived near the vær[1] at winter time, long after the fishing season was over, was a woman and a slip of a girl. Their business was to guard the scaffolding poles for drying fish against the birds of prey, who had such a villainous trick of hacking at the drying-ropes.

The young girl had thick coal-black hair, and a pair of eyes that peeped at folk so oddly. One might almost have

---

1. *Vær*: a fishing-station where fishermen gather periodically.

59

said that she was like the cormorants outside there, and she had never seen much else all her life. Nobody knew who her father was.

Thus they lived till the girl had grown up.

It was found that, in the summertime, when the fishermen went out to the vær to fetch away the dried fish, that the young fellows began underbidding each other, so as to be selected for that special errand.

Some gave up their share of profits, and others their wages, and there was a general complaint in all the villages round about that on such occasions no end of betrothals were broken off.

But the cause of it all was the girl out yonder with the odd eyes.

For all her rough-and-ready ways, she had something about her, said those she chatted with, that there was no resisting. She turned the heads of all the young fellows; it seemed as if they couldn't live without her.

The first winter a lad wooed her who had both house and warehouse of his own.

"If you come again in the summertime, and give me the right gold ring I will be wedded by, something may come of it," she said.

And, sure enough, in the summertime the lad was there again.

He had a lot of fish to fetch away, and she might have had a gold ring as heavy and as bonnie as heart could wish for.

"The ring I must have lies beneath the wreckage in the iron chest, over at the island yonder," said she; "that is, if you love me enough to dare fetch it."

But the lad grew pale.

He saw the sea bore rise and fall out there like a white wall of foam on the bright warm summer day, and on the island sat the cormorants sleeping in the sunshine.

61

"Dearly do I love thee," said he, "but such a quest as that would mean my burial, not my bridal."

The same instant the thirteenth cormorant rose from his stone in the misty foam, and flew right over the island.

Next winter the steersman of a yacht came a wooing. For two years he had gone about and hugged his misery for her sake, and he got the same answer.

"If you come again in the summertime, and give me the right gold ring I will be wedded with, something may come of it."

Out to the vær he came again on Midsummer Day.

But when he heard where the gold ring lay, he sat and wept the whole day till evening, when the sun began to dance north-westward into the sea.

Then the thirteenth cormorant arose, and flew right over the island.

There was nasty weather during the third winter.

There were manifold wrecks, and on the keel of a boat, which came driving ashore, hung an exhausted young lad by his knife belt.

But they couldn't get the life back into him, roll and rub him about in the boathouse as they might.

Then the girl came in.

"'Tis my bridegroom!" said she.

And she laid him in her bosom, and sat with him the whole night through, and put warmth into his heart.

And when the morning came, his heart beat.

"Methought I lay betwixt the wings of a cormorant, and leaned my head against its downy breast," said he.

The lad was ruddy and handsome, with curly hair, and he couldn't take his eyes away from the girl.

He took work upon the vær.

But off he must needs be gadding and chatting with her, be it never so early and never so late.

So it fared with him as it had fared with the others.

It seemed to him that he could not live without her, and on the day when he was bound to depart, he wooed her.

"*Thee* I will not fool," said she. "Thou hast lain on my breast, and I would give my life to save thee from sorrow. Thou shalt have me if thou wilt place the betrothal ring upon my finger, but longer than the day lasts thou canst not keep me. And now I will wait, and long after thee with a horrible longing, till the summer comes."

On Midsummer Day the youth came thither in his boat all alone.

Then she told him of the ring that he must fetch for her from among the skerries.

"If thou has taken me off the keel of a boat, thou mayest cast me forth yonder again," said the lad. "Live without thee I cannot."

But as he laid hold of the oars in order to row out, she stepped into the boat with him and sat in the stern. Wondrous fair was she!

It was beautiful summer weather, and there was a swell upon the sea; wave followed upon wave in long bright rollers.

The lad sat there, lost in the sight of her, and he rowed and rowed till the in-sucking breakers roared and thundered among the skerries; the groundswell was strong, and the frothing foam spurted up as high as towers.

"If thy life is dear to thee, turn back now," said she.

"Thou art dearer to me than life itself," he made answer.

But just as it seemed to the lad as if the prow were going under, and the jaws of death were gaping wide before him, it grew all at once as still as a calm, and the boat could run ashore as if there was never a billow there.

On the island lay a rusty old ship's anchor half out of the sea.

"In the iron chest which lies beneath the anchor is my

dowry," said she. "Carry it up into thy boat, and put the ring that thou seest on my finger. With this thou dost make me thy bride. So now I am thine till the sun dances north-westwards into the sea."

It was a gold ring with a red stone in it, and he put it on her finger and kissed her.

In a cleft on the skerry was a patch of green grass. There they sat them down, and they were ministered to in wondrous wise, how he knew not nor cared to know, so great was his joy.

"Midsummer Day is beauteous," said she, "and I am young and thou art my bridegroom. And now we'll to our bridal bed."

So bonnie was she that he could not contain himself for love.

But when night drew nigh, and the sun began to dance out into the sea, she kissed him and shed tears.

"Beauteous is the summer day," said she, "and still more beauteous is the summer evening, but now the dusk cometh."

And all at once it seemed to him as if she were becoming older and older and fading right away.

When the sun went below the sea margin there lay before him on the skerry some moldering linen rags and naught else.

Calm was the sea, and in the clear midsummer night there flew *twelve* cormorants out over the sea.

"Isaac and the Parson of Brönö"

In Helgeland there was once a fisherman called Isaac. One day when he was out halibut fishing he felt something heavy on the lines. He drew up, and lo, there was a sea boot.

"That *was* a rum'un!" said he, and he sat there a long time looking at it.

It looked just as if it might be the boot of his brother who had gone down in the great storm last winter on his way home from fishing.

There was still something *inside* the boot too, but he durst not look to see what it was, nor did he exactly know what to do with the sea boot either.

He didn't want to take it home and frighten his mother, nor did he quite fancy chucking it back into the sea again; so he made up his mind to go to the parson of Brönö, and beg him to bury it in a Christian way.

"But I can't bury a sea boot," quoth the parson.

The fellow scratched his head. "Na, na!" said he.

Then he wanted to know how much there ought to be of a human body before it could have the benefit of Christian burial.

"That I cannot exactly tell you," said the parson, "a tooth, or a finger, or hair clippings is not enough to read the burial service over. Anyhow, there ought to be so much remaining that one can see that a soul has been in it. But to read Holy Scripture over a toe or two in a sea boot! Oh, no! That would never do!"

But Isaac watched his opportunity, and managed to get

the sea boot into the churchyard on the sly, all the same.

And home he went.

It seemed to him that he had done the best he could. It was better, after all, that *something* of his brother should lie so near God's house than that he should have heaved the boot back into the black sea again.

But, towards autumn, it so happened that, as he lay out among the skerries on the lookout for seals, and the ebb tide drove masses of tangled seaweed towards him, he fished up a knife belt and an empty sheath with his oar blade.

He recognized them at once as his brother's.

The tarred wire covering of the sheath had been loosened and bleached by the sea, and he remembered quite well how, when his brother had sat and cobbled away at this sheath, he had chatted and argued with him about the leather for his belt which he had taken from an old horse which they had lately killed.

They had bought the buckle together over at the storekeeper's on the Saturday, and mother had sold bilberries, and capercailzies, and three pounds of wool. They had got a little tipsy, and had had such fun with the old fishwife at the headland, who had used a bast-mat for a sail.

So he took the belt away with him, and said nothing about it. It was no good giving pain to no purpose, thought he.

But the longer the winter lasted the more he bothered himself with odd notions about what the parson had said. And he knew not what he should do in case he came upon something else, such as another boot, or something that a squid, or a fish, or a crab, or a Greenland shark might have bitten off. He began to be really afraid of rowing out in the sea there among the skerries.

And yet, for all that, it was as though he were constantly being drawn thither by the hope of finding, perhaps, so much of the remains as might show the parson where the soul had been, and so move him to give them a Christian burial.

He took to walking about all by himself in a brown study.

And then, too, he had such nasty dreams.

His door flew open in the middle of the night and let in a cold sea blast, and it seemed to him as if his brother were limping about the room, and yelling that he must have his foot again, the draugs were pulling and twisting him about so.

For hours and hours he stood over his work without laying a hand to it, and blankly staring at the fifth wall[1].

At last he felt as if he were really going out of his wits, because of the great responsibility he had taken upon himself by burying the foot in the churchyard.

He didn't want to pitch it into the sea again, but it couldn't lie in the churchyard either.

It was borne in upon him so clearly that his brother could not be among the blessed, and he kept going about and thinking of all that might be lying and drifting and floating about among the skerries.

So he took it upon himself to dredge there, and lay out by the seashore with ropes and dredging gear. But all that he dredged up was sea wrack, and weeds, and starfish, and like rubbish.

One evening as he sat out there by the rocks trying his luck at fishing, and the line with the stone and all the hooks upon it shot down over the boat's side, the last of the hooks caught in one of his eyes, and right to the bottom went the eye.

There was no use dredging for *that*, and he could see to row home very well without it.

In the night he lay with a bandage over his eye, wake-

---

1. *Fifth wall*: nothing, a house having usually only *four* walls.

ful for pain, and he thought and thought till things looked as black as they could be to him. Was there ever anyone in the world in such a hobble as he?

All at once such an odd thing happened.

He thought he was looking about him, deep down in the sea, and he saw the fishes flitting and snapping about among the sea wrack and seaweed round about the fishing line. They bit at the bait, and wriggled and tried to slip off, first a cod, and then a ling, and then a dogfish. Last of all, a haddock came and stood still there, and chewed the water a little as if it were tasting before swallowing it.

And he saw there what he couldn't take his eyes off. It looked like the back of a man in leather clothes, with one sleeve caught beneath the grapnel of a *femböring*.

Then a heavy white halibut came up and gulped down the hook, and it became pitch dark.

"You must let the big halibut slip off again when you pull up tomorrow," something said, "the hook tears my mouth so. 'Tis of no use searching except in the evening, when the tide in the sound is on ebb."

Next day he went off, and took a piece of a tombstone from the churchyard to dredge the bottom with, and in the evening, when the tide had turned, he lay out in the sound again and searched.

Immediately he hauled up the grapnel of a *femböring*, the hooks of which were clinging to a leather fisherman's jacket, with the remains of an arm in it.

The fishes had got as much as they could of it out of the leather jacket.

Off to the parson he rowed straightway.

"What! Read the service over a washed-out old leather jacket!" cried the parson of Brönö.

"I'll throw the sea boot into the bargain," answered Isaac.

"Waifs and strays and sea salvage should be advertised in the church porch," thundered the parson.

Then Isaac looked straight into the parson's face.

"The sea boot has been heavy enough on my conscience," said he; "and I'm sure I don't want to be saddled with the leather jacket as well."

"I tell you I don't mean to cast consecrated earth to the winds," said the parson; he was getting wroth.

Isaac scratched his head again. "Na, na!" said he.

And with that he had to be content and go home.

But Isaac had neither rest nor repose, there lay such a grievous load upon him.

In the nighttime he again saw the big white halibut. It was going round and round so slowly and sadly in the selfsame circle at the bottom of the sea. It was just as if some invisible sort of netting was all round it, and the whole time it was striving to slip through the meshes.

Isaac lay there, and gazed and gazed till his blind eye ached again.

No sooner was he out dredging next day, and had let down the ropes, than an ugly heavy squid came up, and spouted up a black jet right in front of him.

But one evening he let the boat drive, as the current chose to take it, outside the skerries, but within the islands. At last it stopped at a certain spot, as if it were moored fast, and there it grew wondrously still; there was not a bird in the air or a sign of life in the sea.

All at once up came a big bubble right in front of the jib, and as it burst he heard a deep heavy sigh.

But Isaac had his own opinion about what he had seen.

"And the parson of Brönö shall see to the funeral too, or I'll know the reason why," said he.

From henceforth it was bruited abroad that he had second sight, and saw many things about him which were hidden from other folks.

He could tell exactly where the fish were to be found thick together by the sea banks, and where they were not, and whenever they asked him about such things, he would say—

"If I don't know it, my brother does."

Now one day it chanced that the parson of Brönö had to go out along the coast on a pious errand, and Isaac was one of them who had to row him thither.

Off they went with a rattling good breeze.

The parson got there quickly, and was not very long about his business, for next day he had to hold divine service in his own parish church.

"The firth seems to me a bit roughish," said he, "and 'tis getting towards evening, but as we have come hither, I should think we could get back again also."

They had not got very far on their homeward journey when the rising gale began to whistle and whine, so that they had to take in four clews.

And away they went, with the sea scud and the snowflakes flying about their ears, while the waxing rollers rose big as houses.

The parson of Brönö had never been out in such weather before. They sailed right into the rollers, and they sailed out again.

Soon it became black night.

The sea shone like mountain snow fields, and the showers of snow and spray rather waxed than waned.

Isaac had just taken in the fifth clew also when one of the planks amidships gave way, so that the sea foamed in, and the parson of Brönö and the crew leaped upon the upper deck, and bawled out that the boat was going down.

"I don't think she'll founder this voyage," said Isaac, and he remained sitting where he was at the rudder.

But as the moon peeped forth from behind a hail

shower, they saw that a strange foremastman was standing in the scuppers, and baling water out of the boat as fast as it poured in.

"I didn't know that I had hired that fellow yonder," said the parson of Brönö; "he seems to me to be baling with a sea boot, and it also seems to me as if he had neither breeches nor skin upon his legs, and the upper part of him is neither more nor less than an empty fluttering leather jacket."

"Parson has seen him before, I think," said Isaac.

Then the parson of Brönö grew angry.

"By virtue of my sacred office," said he, "I adjure him to depart from amidships."

"Na, na!" answered Isaac, "and can Parson also answer for the plank that has burst?"

Then the parson bethought him of the evil case he was in.

"The man seems to me mortally strong, and we have great need of him," said he, "nor is it any great sin, methinks, to help a servant of God's over the sea. But I should like to know what he wants in return."

The billows burst, and the blast howled around him.

"Only some two or three shovels of earth on a rotten sea boot and a moldy skin jacket," said Isaac.

"If you're able to gad about again here below, I suppose there's nothing against your being able to enter into bliss again, for all that I know," bawled the parson of Brönö; "and you shall have your shovelfuls of earth into the bargain."

Just as he said this, the water within the skerries all at once became quite smooth, and the parson's boat drove high and dry upon the sandbank, so that the mast cracked.

"The Wind-Gnome"

There was once a skipper of Dyrevig called Bardun. He was so headstrong that there was no doing anything with him. Whatever he set his mind upon, that should be done, he said, and done it always was.

If he promised to be at a dance, the girls could safely rely upon his being there, though it blew a tempest and rained cats and dogs.

He would come scudding along on a *færing*[1] to his father's house through storm and stress. Row upon row of girls would be waiting for him there, and he spanked the floor with every one of them in turn, and left their gallants to cool their heels as best they might.

Cock-of-the-walk he always must be.

He would go shark fishing too, and would venture with his fishing gaff into seas only large vessels were wont to go.

If there was anything nobody else dared do, Bardun was the man to do it. And, absurd and desperate as the venture might be, he always succeeded, so that folks were always talking about him.

Now, right out at sea beyond the skerries, lay a large rock, the lair of wild fowl, whither the merchant who owned it came every year to bring away rich loads of eiderdown. A long way down the side of this lofty rock was a cleft. Nobody could tell how far *into* the rock it went, and so inaccessible was it there that its owner had said that whoever liked might come and take eiderdown from thence. It became quite a proverb to say, when anything couldn't be done, that it was just as impossible as taking

1. *Færing*: A small, two-oared boat.

eiderdown from Dyrevig rock.

But Bardun passed by the rock, and peeped up at the cleft, and saw all the hosts of the fowls of the air lighting upon it so many times that he felt he needs must try his hand at it.

He lost no time about it, and the sun was shining brightly as he set out.

He took with him a long piece of rope, which he cast two or three times round a rocky crag, and lowered himself down till he was right opposite the cleft. There he hung and swung over it backwards and forwards till he had got a firm footing, and then he set about collecting eiderdown and stuffing his sacks with it.

He went searching about for it so far into the rocky chasm that he saw no more than a gleam of sunlight outside the opening, and he couldn't take a hundredth part of the eiderdown that was there.

It was quite late in the evening before he gave up trying to gather it all. But when he came out again, the stone which he had placed on the top of the rope and tied it to was gone. And now the rope hung loosely there, and dangled over the side of the rock. The wind blew it in and out and hither and thither. The currents of air sported madly with it, so that it always kept sheer away from the rock and far out over the abyss.

There he stood then, and tried again and again to clutch hold of it till the sun lay right down in the sea.

When it began to dawn again, and the morning breeze rose up from the sea, he all at once heard something right over his head say—

"It blows away, it blows away!"

He looked up, and there he saw a big woman holding the rope away from the cliff side.

Every time he made a grip at it, she wrenched and twisted it right away over the rocky wall, and there was a laughing and a grinning all down the mountainside—

"It blows away, it blows away!"

And, again and again, the rope drove in and out and hither and thither.

"You had better take a spring at once, and not wait till you're tired," thought he.

It was a pretty long leap to take, but he went back a sufficient distance, and then out he sprang.

Bardun was not a man to fall short of anything. He caught the rope and held it tight.

And, oddly enough, it seemed now to run up the cliff-side of its own accord, just as if someone were hoisting it.

But in front of the rocky crag to which he had fastened the rope, he heard a soughing and a sighing, and something said, "I am the daughter of the Wind-Gnome, and now thou hast dominion over me! When the blast blows and whines about thee 'tis I who long for thee. And here thou hast a rudder which will give thee luck and a fair wind whithersoever thou farest. He who is with thee shall thrive, and he who is against thee shall suffer shipwreck and be lost. For 'tis I who am in the windy gusts."

Then all at once everything was quite still, but down on the sea below there swept a heavy squall.

There stood Bardun with the rudder in his hand, and he understood that it was not a thing to be lightly cast away.

Homeward he steered with a racing breeze behind him, and he had not sailed far before he met a *galeas*[2] which gave him the Bergen price for his eiderdown.

But Bardun was not content with only going thither once. He went just the same as before, and he returned from the Dyrevig rock with a pile of sacks of eiderdown on his boat right up to the mast.

He bought houses and ships; mightier and mightier he

2. *Galeas*: a sailing vessel with a square foresail.

grew.

And it was not long before he owned whole fishing grounds, both northwards and southwards.

Those who submitted to him, and did as he would have them do, increased and prospered, and saw good days, but all who stood in his way were wrecked on the sea and perished, for the Wind-Gnome was on his side.

So things quickly went from good to better with him. What was to him a fair wind was the ruin of all those who were in any way opposed to him. At last he became so rich and mighty that he owned every blessed trading place and fishing station in all Finmark, and sent vessels even as far as Spitzbergen.

Nobody durst sell fish up north without his leave, and his sloops sailed over to Bergen eighteen at a time.

He ruled and gave judgment as it seemed best to him.

But the magistrates thought that such authority was too much for one man to have, and they began to make inquiries, and receive complaints of how he domineered the people.

Next, the magistrates sent him a warning.

"But the right to rule lies in my rudder," thought Bardun to himself.

Then the magistrates summoned him before the tribunal.

Bardun simply whistled contemptuously.

At last matters came to such a pitch that the magistrates sailed forth to seize him in the midst of a howling tempest, and down they went in the Finmark seas.

Then Bardun was made chief magistrate, till such time as the king should send up another.

But the new man who came had not been very long in office there before it seemed to him as if it was not he but Bardun who held sway.

So the same thing happened over again.

Bardun was summoned in vain before the courts, and the magistrates came forth to seize him and perished at sea.

But when the next governor was sent up to Finmark, it was only the keel of the king's ship that came drifting in from the sea. At last nobody would venture thither to certain ruin, and Bardun was left alone, and ruled over all. Then so mighty was he in all Finmark that he reigned there like the king himself.

Now he had but one child, and that a daughter.

Boel was her name, and she shot up so handsome and comely that her beauty shone like the sun. No bridegroom was good enough for her, unless, perhaps, it were the king's son.

Wooers came from afar, and came in vain. She was to have a dower, they said, such as no girl in the North had ever had before.

One year quite a young officer came up thither with a letter from the king. His garments were stiff with gold, and shone and sparkled wherever he went. Bardun received him well, and helped him to carry out the king's commands.

But since the day when he himself was young, and got the answer, "Yes!" from his bride, he had never been so happy as when Boel came to him one day and said that the young officer had wooed her, and she would throw herself into the sea straightway if she couldn't have him.

In this way, he argued, his race would always sit in the seat of authority, and hold sway when he was gone.

While the officer, in the course of the summer, was out on circuit, Bardun set a hundred men to work to build a house for them.

It was to shine like a castle, and be bright with high halls and large reception rooms, and windows in long rooms, and furs and cloth of gold and bright tiles were fetched from the far South.

And in the autumn there was such a wedding that the whole land heard and talked about it.

But it was not long before Bardun began to find that to be a fact which was already a rumor, to wit, that the man who had got his daughter would fain have his own way also.

He laid down the law, and gave judgment like Bardun himself, and he overruled Bardun, not once nor twice.

Then Bardun went to Boel, and bade her take her husband to task, and look sharp about it. He had never yet seen the man, said he, who couldn't be set right by his bride in the days when they did nothing but eat honey together.

But Boel said that she wedded a man who, to her mind, was no less a man than her own father; and it was his office, besides, to uphold the law and jurisdiction of the king.

Young folks are easy to talk over, thought Bardun. One can do anything with them when one only makes them fancy they are having their own way. And it is wonderful how far one can get if one only bides one's time, and makes the best of things. Whatever was out of gear he could very easily put right again, when once he got a firm grip of the reins.

So he praised everything his son-in-law did, and talked big about him, so that there was really no end to it. He was glad, he said, that such a wise and stately ruler was there, ready to stand in his shoes against the day when he should grow old.

And so he made himself small, and his voice quivered when he spoke, as if he were really a sick and broken-down man.

But it didn't escape Boel how he slammed to the doors, and struck the stones with his stick till the sparks flew.

Next time the court met, Bardun was taxed to a full tenth of the value of all his property, according to the king's law and justice.

Then only did he begin to foresee that it might fare with the magistrates now as it had done formerly.

But all women like pomp and show, thought he, and Boel was in this respect no different from other people. And she was no daughter of his either, if she couldn't keep the upper hand of her husband.

So he bought her gold and jewels, and other costly things. One day he came with a bracelet, and another day with a chain, and now it was a belt, and now a gold embroidered shoe. And every time he told her that he brought her these gifts, because she was his dearest jewel. He knew of nothing in the world that was too precious for her.

Then, in his most pleasant, most courtly style, he just hinted that she might see to it, and talk her husband over to other ways.

But it booted him even less than before.

And so things went on till autumn. The king's law was first, and his will was only second.

Then he began to dread what would be the end of it all. His eyes sparkled so fiercely that none dare come near him. But at night he would pace up and down, and shriek and bellow at his daughter, and give her all sorts of vile names.

Now one day he came in to Boel with a heavy gold crown full of the most precious stones. She should be the Queen of Finmark and Spitzbergen, said he, if her husband would do according to his will.

Then she looked him stiffly in the face, and said she would never seduce her husband into breaking the king's law.

He grew pale as the wall behind him, and cast the gold

crown on the floor, so that there was a perfect shower of precious stones about them.

She must know, said he, that her father and none other was king here. And now the young officer should find out how it fared with them who sat in his seat.

Then Boel washed her hands of her father altogether, but she advised her husband to depart forthwith.

And on the third day she had packed up all her bridal finery, and departed in the vessel with the young officer.

Then Bardun smote his head against the wall, and that night he laughed, so that it was heard far away, but he wept for his daughter.

And now there arose such a storm that the sea was white for a whole week. And it was not long before the tidings came that the ship that Boel and her husband had sailed by had gone down, and the splinters lay and floated among the skerries.

Then Bardun took the rudder he had got from the Wind-Gnome, and stuck it into the stern of the largest yacht he had. He was God himself now, said he, and could always get a fair wind to steer by, and could rule where he would in the wide world. And southwards he sailed with a rattling breeze, and the billows rolled after him like mounds and hillocks.

Heavier and heavier grew the sea, till it rolled like white mountains as high as the rocky walls of Lofoten.

It couldn't well be less when he was to rule the whole world, cried he. And so he set his rudder dead southwards.

He never diminished his sail one bit, and worse and worse grew the storm, and higher and higher rose the sea.

For now he was steering right into the sun.

The Huldrefish

It was such an odd trout that Nona hauled in at the end of his fishing line. Large and fat, red, spotted and shiny, it sprawled and squirmed, with its dirty yellow belly above the water, to wriggle off the hook. And when he got it into the boat, and took it off the hook, he saw that it had only two small slits where the eyes should have been.

It must be a huldrefish[1], thought one of the boatsmen, for rumor had it that that lake was one of those which had a double bottom.

But Nona didn't trouble his head very much about what sort of fish it was, so long as it was a big one. He was ravenously hungry, and bawled to them to row as rapidly as possible ashore so as to get it cooked.

He had been sitting the whole afternoon with empty lines out in the mountain lake there, but as for the trout, it was only an hour ago since it had been steering its way through the water with its rudder of a tail, and allowed itself to be fooled by a hook, and already it lay cooked red there on the dish.

But now Nona recollected about the strange eyes, and felt for them, and pricked away at its head with his fork. There was nothing but slits outside, and yet there was a sort of hard eyeball inside. The head was strangely shaped, and looked very peculiar in many respects.

He was vexed that he had not examined it more closely before it was cooked; it was not so easy now to make out what it really was. It had tasted first-rate, however, and that was something.

1. *Hulder, huldre*, a name for anything elfin or gnomish. Compare *Ice. Hulda*, a hiding, covering. It implies the invisibility of the elfin race.

But at night there was, as it were, a gleam of bright water before his eyes, and he lay half asleep, thinking of the odd fish he had pulled up.

He was in his boat again, he thought, and it seemed to him as if his hands felt the fish wriggling and sprawling for its life, and shooting its snout backwards and forwards to get off the hook.

All at once it grew so heavy and strong that it drew the boat after it by the line.

It went along at a frightful speed, while the lake gradually diminished, as it were, and dried up.

There was an irresistible sucking of the water in the direction the fish went, which was towards a hole at the bottom of the lake like a funnel, and right into this hole went the boat.

It glided for a long time in a sort of twilight along a subterranean river, which dashed and splashed about him. The air that met him was, at first, chilly and cellar-like; gradually, however, it grew milder and milder, and warmer and warmer.

The stream now flowed along calmly and quietly, and broadened out continually till it fell into a large lake.

Beyond the borders of this lake, but only half visible in the gloom, stretched swamps and morasses, where he heard sounds as of huge beasts wading and trampling. Serpent-like they rose and writhed with a crashing and splashing and snorting amidst the tepid mud and mire.

By the phosphorescent gleams he saw various fishes close to his boat, but all of them lacked eyes.

And he caught glimpses of the outlines of gigantic sea serpents stretching far away into the darkness. He now understood that it was from down here that they pop up their heads off the coast in the dog days when the sea is warm.

The lindworm, with its flat head and duck's beak,

darted after fish, and crept up to the surface of the earth through the slimy ways of mire and marsh.

Through the warm and choking gloom there came, from time to time, a cooling chilling blast from the cold curves and winds of the slimy and slippery greenish lich-worm[2], which bores its way through the earth and eats away the coffins that are rotting in the churchyards.

Horrible, shapeless monsters, with streaming manes, such as are said to sometimes appear in mountain tarns, writhed and wallowed and seized their prey in the fens and marshes.

And he caught glimpses of all sorts of human-like creatures, such as fishermen and sailors meet and marvel at on the sea, and landsmen see outside the elfin mounds.

And, besides that, there was a soft whizzing and an endless hovering and swarming of beings, whose shapes were nevertheless invisible to the eye of man.

Then the boat glided into miry pulpy water, where her course tended downwards, and where the earth vault above darkened as it sank lower and lower.

All at once a blinding strip of light shot down from a bright blue slit high, high above him.

A stuffy vapor stood round about him. The water was as yellow and turbid as that which comes out of steam boilers.

And he called to mind the peculiar tepid undrinkable water which bubbles up by the side of artesian wells. It was quite hot. Up there they were boring down to a world of warm watercourses and liquid strata beneath the earth's crust.

Heat as from an oven rose up from the huge abysses and dizzying clefts, whilst mighty steaming waterfalls roared and shook the ground.

All at once he felt as if his body were breaking loose,

2. Lichworm, a serpent that eats the dead. If we have Lichfield and lichgate, we may have lichworm too.

freeing itself, and rising into the air. He had a feeling of infinite lightness, of a wondrous capability for floating in higher atmospheres and recovering equilibrium.

And, before he knew how it was, he found himself up on the earth again.

FINN BLOOD

Finn Blood

In Svartfjord, north of Senje, dwelt a lad called Eilert. His neighbors were seafaring Finns, and among their children was a pale little girl, remarkable for her long black hair and her large eyes. They dwelt behind the crag on the other side of the promontory, and fished for a livelihood, as also did Eilert's parents; wherefore there was no particular goodwill between the families, for the nearest fishing ground was but a small one, and each would have liked to have rowed there alone.

Nevertheless, though his parents didn't like it at all, and even forbade it, Eilert used to sneak regularly down to the Finns. There they had always strange tales to tell, and he heard wondrous things about the recesses of the mountains, where the original home of the Finns was, and where, in the olden time, dwelt the Finn kings, who were masters among the magicians. There, too, he heard tell of all that was beneath the sea, where the mermen and the draugs hold sway. The latter are gloomy evil powers, and many a time his blood stood still in his veins as he sat and listened. They told him that the draug usually showed himself on the strand in the moonlight on those spots which were covered with sea wrack, that he had a bunch of seaweed instead of a head, but shaped so peculiarly that whoever came across him absolutely couldn't help gazing into his pale and horrible face. They themselves had seen him many a time, and once they had driven him, thwart by thwart, out of the boat where he had sat one morning, and turned the oars upside down. When Eilert hastened homewards in the darkness round the headland, along the strand, over heaps of seaweed, he dare scarcely look around him, and many a time the sweat absolutely streamed from his forehead.

In proportion as hostility increased among the old people, they had a good deal of fault to find with one another, and Eilert heard no end of evil things spoken about the Finns at home. Now it was this, and now it was that. They didn't even row like honest folk, for, after the Finnish fashion, they took high and swift strokes, as if they were womenkind, and they all talked together, and made a noise while they rowed, instead of being "silent in the boat." But what impressed Eilert most of all was the fact that, in the Finnwoman's family, they practiced sorcery and idolatry, or so folks said. He also heard tell of something beyond all question, and that was the shame of having Finn blood in one's veins, which also was the reason why the Finns were not as good as other honest folk, so that the magistrates gave them their own distinct burial ground in the churchyard, and their own separate "Finn-pens" in the church. Eilert had seen this with his own eyes in church at Berg.

All this made him very angry, for he could not help liking the Finn folks down yonder, and especially little Zilla. They two were always together; she knew such a lot about the Merman. Henceforth his conscience always plagued him when he played with her, and whenever she stared at him with her large black eyes while she told him tales, he used to begin to feel a little bit afraid, for at such times he reflected that she and her people belonged to the Damned, and that was why they knew so much about such things. But, on the other hand, the thought of it made him so bitterly angry, especially on her account. She, too, was frequently taken aback by his odd behavior towards her, which she couldn't understand at all, and then, as was her wont, she would begin laughing at and teasing him by making him run after her, while she went and hid herself.

One day he found her sitting on a boulder by the seashore. She had in her lap an eider duck which had been shot, and could only have died quite recently, for it was still warm, and she wept bitterly over it. It was, she sobbed, the same bird which made its nest every year beneath the shelter of their outhouse—she knew it quite well, and she showed him a red-colored feather in its white breast. It had been struck dead by a single shot, and only a single red drop had come out of it; it had tried to reach its nest, but had died on its way on the strand. She wept as if her heart would break, and dried her face with her hair in impetuous Finnish fashion. Eilert laughed at her as boys will, but he overdid it, and was very pale the whole time. He dared not tell her that that very day he had taken a random shot with his father's gun from behind the headland at a bird a long way off which was swimming ashore.

One autumn Eilert's father was downright desperate. Day after day on the fishing grounds his lines caught next to nothing, while he was forced to look on and see the Finn pull up one rich catch after another. He was sure, too, that he had noticed malicious gestures over in the Finn's boat. After that his whole house nourished a double bitterness against them, and when they talked it over in the evening, it was agreed, as a thing beyond all question, that Finnish sorcery had something to do with it. Against this there was only one remedy, and that was to rub corpse mold on the lines, but one must beware of doing so, lest one should thereby offend the dead, and expose oneself to their vengeance, while the sea folk would gain power over one at the same time.

Eilert bothered his head a good deal over all this; it almost seemed to him as if he had had a share in the deed, because he was on such a good footing with the Finn folks.

On the following Sunday, both he and the Finn folks

were at Berg church, and he secretly abstracted a handful of mold from one of the Finn graves, and put it in his pocket. The same evening, when they came home, he strewed the mold over his father's lines unobserved. And, oddly enough, the very next time his father cast his lines, as many fish were caught as in the good old times. But after this Eilert's anxiety became indescribable. He was especially cautious while they were working of an evening round the fireside, and it was dark in the distant corners of the room. He sat there with a piece of steel in his pocket. To "beg forgiveness" of the dead is the only helpful means against the consequences of such deeds as his, otherwise one will be dragged off at night by an invisible hand to the churchyard, though one were lashed fast to the bed by a ship's hawser.

When Eilert, on the following "Preaching Sunday," went to church, he took very good care to go to the grave, and beg forgiveness of the dead.

As Eilert grew older, he got to understand that the Finn folks must, after all, be pretty much the same sort of people as his own folks at home, but, on the other hand, another thought was now uppermost in his mind, the thought, namely, that the Finns must be of an inferior stock, with a taint of disgrace about them. Nevertheless, he could not very well do without Zilla's society, and they were very much together as before, especially at the time of their confirmation.

But when Eilert became a man, and mixed more with the people of the parish, he began to fancy that this old companionship lowered him somewhat in the eyes of his neighbors. There was nobody who did not believe as a matter of course that there was something shameful about Finn blood, and he, therefore, always tried to avoid her in company.

The girl understood it all well enough, for latterly she

took care to keep out of his way. Nevertheless, one day she came, as had been her wont from childhood, down to their house, and begged for leave to go in their boat when they rowed to church next day. There were lots of strangers present from the village, and so Eilert, lest folks should think that he and she were engaged, answered mockingly, so that everyone could hear him, "that church-cleansing was perhaps a very good thing for Finnish sorcery," but she must find someone else to ferry her across.

After that she never spoke to him at all, but Eilert was anything but happy in consequence.

Now it happened one winter that Eilert was out all alone fishing for Greenland shark. A shark suddenly bit. The boat was small, and the fish was very big, but Eilert would not give in, and the end of the business was that his boat capsized.

All night long he lay on the top of it in the mist and a cruel sea. As now he sat there almost fainting for drowsiness, and dimly conscious that the end was not far off, and the sooner it came the better, he suddenly saw a man in seaman's clothes sitting astride the other end of the boat's bottom, and glaring savagely at him with a pair of dull reddish eyes. He was so heavy that the boat's bottom began to slowly sink down at end where he sat. Then he suddenly vanished, but it seemed to Eilert as if the sea fog lifted a bit; the sea had all at once grown quite calm (at least, there was now only a gentle swell), and right in front of him lay a little low gray island, towards which the boat was slowly drifting.

The skerry was wet, as if the sea had only recently been flowing over it, and on it he saw a pale girl with such lovely eyes. She wore a green kirtle, and round her body a broad silver girdle with figures upon it, such as the Finns use. Her bodice was of tar-brown skin, and beneath her stay-laces, which seemed to be of green sea grass, was a foam-white chemise, like the feathery breast of a sea bird.

When the boat came drifting onto the island, she came down to him and said, as if she knew him quite well, "So you're come at last, Eilert; I've been waiting for you so long!"

It seemed to Eilert as if an icy cold shudder ran through his body when he took the hand which helped him ashore, but it was only for the moment, and he forgot it instantly.

In the midst of the island there was an opening with a brazen flight of steps leading down to a splendid cabin. Whilst he stood there thinking things over a bit, he saw two heavy dogfish swimming close by—they were, at least, twelve to fourteen ells[1] long.

As they descended, the dogfish sank down too, each on one side of the brazen steps. Oddly enough, it looked as if the island was transparent. When the girl perceived that he was frightened, she told him that they were only two of her father's bodyguards, and shortly afterwards they disappeared. She then said that she wanted to take him to her father, who was waiting for them. She added that, if he didn't find the old gentleman precisely as handsome as he might expect, he had, nevertheless, no need to be frightened, nor was he to be astonished too much at what he saw.

He now perceived that he was under water, but, for all that, there was no sign of moisture. He was on a white sandy bottom, covered with chalk-white, red, blue, and silvery-bright shells. He saw meadows of sea grass, mountains thick with woods of bushy seaweed and sea wrack, and the fishes darted about on every side just as the birds swarm about the rocks that seafowl haunt.

As they two were walking along together, she explained many things to him. High up he saw something

1. Ell: a unit of measurement, different in different countries, ranging from twenty-seven to forty-five inches.

which looked like a black cloud with a white lining, and beneath it moved backwards and forwards a shape resembling one of the dogfish.

"What you see there is a vessel," said she. "There's nasty weather up there now, and beneath the boat goes he who was sitting along with you on the bottom of the boat just now. If it is wrecked, it will belong to us, and then you will not be able to speak to father today." As she said this there was a wild rapacious gleam in her eyes, but it was gone again immediately.

And, in point of fact, it was no easy matter to make out the meaning of her eyes. As a rule, they were unfathomably dark with the luster of a night-billow through which the sea fire sparkles, but, occasionally, when she laughed, they took a bright sea-green glitter, as when the sun shines deep down into the sea.

Now and again they passed by a boat or a vessel half buried in the sand, out and in of the cabin doors and windows of which fishes swam to and fro. Close by the wrecks wandered human shapes which seemed to consist of nothing but blue smoke. His conductress explained to him that these were the spirits of drowned men who had not had Christian burial—one must beware of them, for dead ones of this sort are malignant. They always know when one of their own race is about to be wrecked, and at such times they howl the death warning of the draug through the wintry nights.

Then they went further on their way right across a deep dark valley. In the rocky walls above him, he saw a row of four-cornered white doors, from which a sort of glimmer as from the northern lights, shot downwards through the darkness. This valley stretched in a northeastwardly direction right under Finmark, she said, and inside the white doors dwelt the old Finn Kings who had perished on the sea. Then she went and opened the nearest of these doors—here, down in the salt ocean, was the last of the kings, who had capsized in the very breeze that he himself had conjured forth, but could not afterwards quell. There, on a block of stone, sat a wrinkled yellow Finn with running eyes and a polished dark-red crown. His large head rocked backwards and forwards on his withered neck, as if it were in the swirl of an ocean current. Beside him, on the same block, sat a still more shriveled and yellow little woman, who also had a crown on, and her garments were covered with all sorts of colored stones; she was stirring up a brew with a stick. If she only had fire beneath it, the girl told Eilert, she and her husband would very soon have dominion again over the salt sea, for the thing she was stirring about was magic stuff.

In the middle of a plain, which opened right before them at a turn of the road, stood a few houses together like a little town, and, a little further on, Eilert saw a church turned upside down, looking, with its long pointed tower, as if it were mirrored in the water. The girl explained to him that her father dwelt in these houses, and the church was one of the seven that stood in his realm, which extended all over Helgeland and Finmark. No service was held in them yet, but it would be held when the drowned bishop, who sat outside in a brown study, could only hit upon the name of the Lord that was to be served, and then all the draugs would go to church. The bishop, she said, had been sitting and pondering the matter over these eight-hundred years, so he would no doubt very soon get to the bottom of it. A hundred years ago the bishop had advised them to send up one of the draugs to Rödö church to find out all about it, but every time the word he wanted was mentioned he couldn't catch the sound of it. In the mountain "Kunnan," King Olaf had hung a high church bell of pure gold, and it is guarded by the first priest who ever came to Nordland, who stands there in a white chasuble. On the day the priest rings the bell, Kunnan will become a big stone church, to which all Nordland, both above and below the sea, will resort. But time flies, and therefore all who come down here below are asked by the bishop if they can tell him that name.

At this Eilert felt very queer indeed, and he felt queerer still when he began reflecting and found, to his horror, that he also had forgotten that name.

While he stood there in thought, the girl looked at him so anxiously. It was almost as if she wanted to help him to find it and couldn't, and with that she all at once grew deadly pale.

The draug's house, to which they now came, was built of boat's keels and large pieces of wreckage, in the interstices of which grew all sorts of sea grass and slimy green stuff. Three monstrously heavy green posts, covered with shellfish, formed the entrance, and the door consisted of planks which had sunk to the bottom and were full of clincher nails. In the middle of it, like a knocker, was a heavy rusty iron mooring ring, with the worn-away stump of a ship's hawser hanging to it. When they came up to it, a large black arm stretched out and opened the door.

They were now in a vaulted chamber, with fine shell-sand on the floor. In the corners lay all sorts of ropes, yarn, and boating gear, and among them casks and barrels and various ship's inventories. On a heap of yarn, covered by an old red-patched sail, Eilert saw the draug, a broad-shouldered, strongly built fellow, with a glazed hat shoved back onto the top of his head, with dark red, tangled hair and beard, small tearful dogfish eyes, and a broad mouth, round which there lay for the moment a good-natured sea-man's grin. The shape of his head reminded one somewhat of the big sort of seal which is called *klakkekal*—his skin about the neck looked dark and shaggy, and the tops of his fingers grew together. He sat there with turned-down sea boots on, and his thick gray woolen stockings reached right up to his thigh. He wore besides, plain frieze clothes with bright glass buttons on his waistcoat. His spacious skin jacket was open, and round his neck he had a cheap red, woolen scarf.

When Eilert came up, he made as if he would rise, and said good naturedly, "Good day, Eilert—you've certainly had a hard time of it today! Now you can sit down, if you like, and take a little grub. You want it, I'm sure." And with that he squirted out a jet of tobacco juice like the spouting of a whale. With one foot, which for that special purpose all at once grew extraordinarily long, he fished out of a corner, in true Nordland style, the skull of a whale to serve as a chair for Eilert, and shoved forward with his hand a long ship's drawer full of first-rate fare. There were boiled groats with syrup, cured fish, oatcakes with butter, a large stack of flatcakes, and a multitude of the best hotel dishes besides.

The Merman bade him fall to and eat his fill, and ordered his daughter to bring out the last keg of Thronhjem *aqua vitæ*. "Of that sort the last is always the best," said he. When she came with it, Eilert thought he knew it again: it was his father's, and he himself, only a couple of days before, had bought the brandy from the wholesale dealer at Kvæford, but he didn't say anything about that now. The quid of tobacco, too, which the draug turned somewhat impatiently in his mouth before he drank, also seemed to him wonderfully like the lead on his own line. At first it seemed to him as if he didn't quite know how to manage with the keg—his mouth was so sore, but afterwards things went along smoothly enough.

So they sat for some time pretty silently, and drank glass after glass, till Eilert began to think that they had had quite enough. So, when it came to his turn again, he said no, he would rather not; whereupon the Merman put the keg to his own mouth and drained it to the very dregs. Then he stretched his long arm up to the shelf, and took down another. He was now in a better humor, and began to talk of all sorts of things. But every time he laughed, Eilert felt queer, for the draug's mouth gaped ominously wide, and showed a greenish pointed row of teeth, with a long interval between each tooth, so that they resembled a row of boat stakes.

The Merman drained keg after keg, and with every keg he grew more communicative. With an air as if he were thinking in his own mind of something very funny, he looked at Eilert for a while and blinked his eyes. Eilert didn't like his expression at all, for it seemed to him to say: "Now, my lad, whom I have fished up so nicely, look out for a change!" But instead of that he said, "You had a rough time of it last night, Eilert, my boy, but it wouldn't have gone so hard with you if you hadn't streaked the lines with corpse mold, and refused to take my daughter to church." Here he suddenly broke off, as if he had said too much, and to prevent himself from completing the sentence, he put the brandy keg to his mouth once more. But the same instant Eilert caught his glance, and it was so full of deadly hatred that it sent a shiver right down his back.

When, after a long, long draught, he again took the keg from his mouth, the Merman was again in a good humor, and told tale after tale. He stretched himself more and more heavily out on the sail, and laughed and grinned complacently at his own narrations, the humor of which was always a wreck or a drowning. From time to time Eilert felt the breath of his laughter, and it was like a cold blast. If folks would only give up their boats, he said, he had no very great desire for the crews. It was driftwood and ship timber that he was after, and he really couldn't get on without them. When his stock ran out, boat or ship he *must* have, and surely nobody could blame him for it either.

With that he put the keg down empty, and became somewhat more gloomy again. He began to talk about what bad times they were for him and her. It was not as it used to be, he said. He stared blankly before him for a time, as if buried in deep thought. Then he stretched himself out backwards at full length, with feet extending right across the floor, and gasped so dreadfully that his upper and lower jaws resembled two boats' keels facing each other. Then he dozed right off with his neck turned towards the sail.

Then the girl again stood by Eilert's side, and bade him follow her.

They now went the same way back, and again ascended up to the skerry. Then she confided to him that the reason why her father had been so bitter against him was because he had mocked her with the taunt about the church-cleansing when she had wanted to go to church— the name the folks down below wanted to know might, the Merman thought, be treasured up in Eilert's memory, but during their conversation on their way down to her father, she had perceived that he also had forgotten it. And now he must look to his life.

It would be a good deal later on in the day before the old fellow would begin inquiring about him. Till then he, Eilert, must sleep so as to have sufficient strength for his flight—she would watch over him.

The girl flung her long dark hair about him like a curtain, and it seemed to him that he knew those eyes so well. He felt as if his cheek were resting against the breast of a white sea-bird, it was so warm and sleep-giving—a single reddish feather in the middle of it recalled a dark memory. Gradually he sank off into a doze, and heard her singing a lullaby, which reminded him of the swell of the billows when it ripples up and down along the beach on a fine sunny day. It was all about how they had once been play-mates together, and how later on he would have nothing to say to her. Of all she sang, however, he could only recollect the last words, which were these:

"Oh, thousands of times have we played by the shore,
And caught little fishes—dost mind it no more?
We raced with the surf as it rolled at our feet,
And the lurking old Merman we always did cheat.

Yes, much shalt thou think of at my lullaby,
Whilst the billows do rock and the breezes do sigh.
Who sits now and weeps o'er thy cheeks? It is she
Who gave thee her soul, and whose soul lived in thee.

But once as an eider duck homeward I came
Thou didst lie 'neath a rock, with thy rifle didst aim;
In my breast thou didst strike me;
       the blood thou dost see
Is the mark that I bear, oh! Beloved one, of thee."

Then it seemed to Eilert as if she sat and wept over him, and that, from time to time, a drop like a splash of sea water fell upon his cheek. He felt now that he loved her so dearly.

The next moment he again became uneasy. He fancied that right up to the skerry came a whale, which said that he, Eilert, must now make haste, and when he stood on its back he stuck the shaft of an oar down its nostril, to prevent it from shooting beneath the sea again. He perceived that in this way the whale could be steered accordingly as he turned the oar to the right or left, and now they coasted the whole land of Finmark at such a rate that the huge mountain islands shot by them like little rocks. Behind him he saw the draug in his half-boat, and he was going so swiftly that the foam stood mid-mast high. Shortly afterwards he was again lying on the skerry, and the lass smiled so blithely; she bent over him and said, "It is I, Eilert."

With that he awoke, and saw that the sunbeams were running over the wet skerry, and the Mermaid was still sitting by his side. But presently the whole thing changed before his eyes. It was the sun shining through the window panes on a bed in the Finn's hut, and by his side sat the Finn girl supporting his back, for they thought he was about to die. He had lain there delirious for six weeks, ever since the Finn had rescued him after capsizing, and this was his first moment of consciousness.

After that it seemed to him that he had never heard anything so absurd and presumptuous as the twaddle that would fix a stigma of shame or contempt on Finn blood, and the same spring he and the Finn girl Zilla were betrothed, and in the autumn they were married.

There were Finns in the bridal procession, and perhaps many said a little more about that than they need have done, but everyone at the wedding agreed that the fiddler, who was also a Finn, was the best fiddler in the whole parish, and the bride the prettiest girl.

The Homestead Westward in the Blue Mountains

There was once a farmer's son who was off to Moen for the annual maneuvers. He was to be the drummer, and his way lay right across the mountains. There he could practice his drumming at his ease, and beat his tattoos again and again without making folks laugh, or having a parcel of small boys dangling about him like so many midges.

Every time he passed a mountain homestead he beat his rat-tat-tat to bring the girls out, and they stood and hung about and gaped after him at all the farmhouses.

It was in the midst of the hottest summer weather. He had been practicing his drumming from early in the morning, till he had grown quite sick and tired of it. And now he was toiling up a steep cliff, and had slung his drum over his shoulder, and stuck his drumsticks in his bandoleer.

The sun baked and broiled upon the hills, but in the clefts there was a coolness as of a rushing roaring waterfall. The little knolls swarmed with bilberries the whole way along, and he felt he must stoop down and pluck whole handfuls at a time, so that it took a long time to get to the top.

Then he came to a hilly slope where the ferns stood high, and there were lots of birch bushes. It was so nice and shady there, he thought, and so he couldn't for the life of him help taking a rest.

His drum he took off, his jacket he put beneath his head, and his cap over his face, and off he went to sleep.

But as he lay dozing there, he dreamt that someone was tickling him under the nose with a straw so that he could get no peace, and the instant he awoke, he fancied he heard laughing and giggling.

The sun had by this time begun to cast oblique shadows, and far down below, towards the valleys, lay the warm steaming vapors, creeping upwards in long drawn-out gossamer bands and ribbons of mist.

As he reached behind him for his jacket, he saw a snake, which lay and looked at him with such shrewd quick eyes. But when he threw a stone at it, it caught its tail in its mouth, and trundled away like a wheel.

Again there was a giggling and a sniggering among the bushes.

And now he heard it among some birch trees which stood in such a wonderful sunlight, for they were filled with the rain and fine drizzle of a waterfall. The water drops glistened and sparkled so that he really couldn't see the trees properly.

But it was as though something were moving about in them, and he could have sworn that he had caught a glimpse of a fine bright slim damsel, who was laughing and making fun of him. She peeped at him from beneath her hand, because of the sun, and her sleeves were tucked up.

A little while afterwards a dark blue blouse appeared above the brushwood.

He was after it in an instant.

He ran and ran till he had half a mind to give up, but then a frock and a bare shoulder gleamed betwixt an opening in the leaves.

And off again he pelted as hard as he could, till he began to think that it must have all been imagination.

Then he saw her right in a corner of the green bushes. Her hair had been torn out of its plaits from the speed with which she had flown through the bushes. She stood still, and looked back as if she were terribly frightened.

But the lad thought to himself that if she had run away with his drumsticks, she should pay for it.

And off they ran again, she in front, and he behind.

Now and again she turned round and laughed and gibed, and gave a toss and a twist, so that it looked as if her long wavy hair were writhing and wriggling and twisting like a serpent's tail.

At last she turned round on the top of the hill, laughed, and held out his drumsticks towards him.

But now he was determined to catch her. He was so near that he made grab after grab at her; but just as he was about to lay hold of her hard by a fence, she was over it, while he tumbled after her into the enclosure of a homestead.

Then she cried and shouted up to the house, "Randi, and Brandi, and Gyri, and Gunna!"

And four girls came rushing down over the sward.

But the last of them, who had a fine ruddy complexion and heavy golden-red hair, stood and greeted him so graciously with her downcast eyes, as if she was quite distressed that they should play such wanton pranks with a strange young man.

She stood there abashed and uncertain, poor thing! Just like a child, who knows not whether it should say something or not, but all the while she sidled up nearer and nearer to him. Then, when she was so close to him that her hair almost touched him, she opened her blue eyes wide, and looked straight at him.

But she had a frightfully sharp look in those eyes of hers.

"Rather come with me, and thou shalt have dancing— or art thou tired, my lad?" cried a girl with blue-black hair, and a wild dark fire in her eyes. She tripped up and down, and clapped her hands. She had white teeth and hot breath, and would have dragged him off with her.

"Tie thyself up behind first, black Gyri!" giggled the others.

And immediately she let the lad go, and wobbled and twisted, and went backwards so oddly.

He couldn't help staring after the black lassie, who stood and writhed and twisted so uncomfortably, as if she were concealing something behind her, and had, all at once, become so meek.

But the fine bright girl with the slim slender waist, who had rushed on before him, and who seemed to him the loveliest of them all, began to laugh at him again and tease him.

Run as he might, he shouldn't catch her, she jibed and jeered; never should he find his drumsticks again, she said.

But then her mood shifted right round, and she flung herself down headlong, and began to cry. She had followed his drumming the whole day, she said, and never had she heard any fellow who could beat rat-tat-tat so well; nor had she ever seen a lad who was so handsome while he was asleep. "I kissed thee then," said she, and smiled up at him sorrowfully.

"Beware of the serpent's tongue, lest it bite thee, swain! 'Tis worst of all when it licks thee first," whispered the bashful one with the golden-red hair. She would fain have stolen between them so softly.

And all at once the swain recollected the snake, which was as slender, and supple, and quick, and sparkling as the girl who lay there on the hillside, and wept and made fun at the same time and looked oddly alert and wary.

But a stooping, somewhat clumsy little thing now stuck her head quickly in between, and smiled shame-facedly at him, as if she knew and could tell him so much.

Her eyes sparkled a long way inwards, and across her face there passed a sort of pale golden gleam, as when the last sunbeam slowly draws away from the grassy mountain slope.

"At my place," said she, "thou shalt hear such *langelejk*[1] as none else has ever heard. I will play for thee, and thou shalt listen to things unknown to others. Thou shalt hear all that sings, and laughs, and cries in the roots of trees, and in the mountains, and in all things that grow, so that thou wilt never trouble thy head about anything else in the world."

Then there was a scornful laugh, and up on a rock he saw a tall strongly built girl, with a gold band in her hair and a huge wand in her hand.

She lifted a long wooden trumpet with such splendid powerful arms, threw back her neck with such a proud and resolute air, and stood firm and fast as a rock while she blew.

And it sounded far and wide through the summer evening, and rang back again across the hills.

But she, the prettiest and daintiest of them all, who had cast herself on the ground, stuck her fingers in her ears, and mimicked her and laughed and jeered.

Then she glanced up at him with her blue eyes peeping through her ashen-yellow hair, and whispered—

"If thou dost want me, swain, thou must pick me up."

"She has a strong firm grip for a gentle maiden," thought he to himself, as he raised her from the ground.

"But thou must catch me first," cried she.

And right towards the house they ran—she first, and he after her.

Suddenly she stopped short, and putting both arms akimbo, looked straight into his eyes: "Dost like me?" she asked.

1. *Langelejk*: A long slow dance, and the music to it.

The swain couldn't say no to that. He had now got hold of her, and would have put his arm round her.

"'Tis for thee to have a word in the matter, Father," she shouted all at once in the direction of the house, "this swain here would fain wed me."

And she drew him hastily towards the hut door.

There sat a little gray-clad old fellow, with a cap like a milk can on his head, staring at the livestock on the mountainside. He had a large silver jug in front of him.

"'Tis the homestead westward in the Blue Mountains that he's after, I know," said the old man, nodding his head, with a sly look in his eyes.

"Haw, haw! That's what they're after, is it?" thought the swain. But aloud he said, "'Tis a great offer, I know, but methinks 'tis a little hasty too. Down our way 'tis the custom to send two go-betweens first of all to arrange matters properly."

"Thou *didst* send two before thee, and here they be," quoth she smartly, and produced his drumsticks.

"And 'tis usual with us, moreover, to have a look over the property first; though the lass herself have wit enough and to spare," added he.

Then she all at once grew so small, and there was a nasty green glitter in her eyes—

"Hast thou not run after me the livelong day, and wooed me right down in the enclosure there, so that my father both heard and saw it all?" cried she.

"Pretty lasses are wont to hold back a bit," said the swain, in a wheedling sort of way. He perceived that he must be a little subtle here; it was not all love in this wooing.

Then she seemed to bend her body backwards into a complete curve, and shot forward her head and neck, and her eyes sparkled.

But the old fellow lifted his stick from his knee, and

she stood there again as blithe and sportive as ever.

She stretched herself out tall and stiff, with her hands in her silver girdle, and she looked right into his eyes and laughed, and asked him if he was one of those fellows who were afraid of the girls. If he wanted her he might perchance be run off his legs again, said she.

Then she began tripping up and down, and curtseying and making fun of him again.

But all at once he saw on the sward behind her what looked like the shadow of something that whisked and frisked and writhed round and round, and twisted in and out according as she practiced her wheedling ways upon him.

"That is a very curious long sort of ribbon," thought the drummer to himself in his amazement. They were in a great hurry, too, to get him under the yoke, he thought, but they should find that a soldier on his way to the maneuvers is not to be betrothed and married offhand.

So he told them bluntly that he had come hither for his drumsticks, and not to woo maidens, and he would thank them to let him have his property.

"But have a look about you a bit first, young man," said the old fellow, and he pointed with his stick.

And all at once the drummer saw large dun cows grazing all along the mountain pastures, and the cowbells rang out their merry peals. Buckets and vats of the brightest copper shone all about, and never had he seen such shapely and nicely dressed milkmaids. There must needs be great wealth here.

"Perchance thou dost think 'tis but a beggarly inheritance I have here in the Blue Mountains," said she, and sitting down on a haycock, she began chatting with him. "But we've four such *sætar*[2] as this, and what I inherit from my mother is twelve times as large."

2. A *Sætar* (Swede. *säter*) is a remote pasturage with huts upon it, where the cows are tended and dairy produce prepared for market and home use during the summer.

But the drummer had seen what he had seen. They were rather too anxious to settle the property upon him, thought he. So he declared that in so serious a matter he must crave a little time for consideration.

Then the lass began to cry and carry on, and asked him if he meant to befool a poor innocent, ignorant, young thing, and pursue her and drive her out of her very wits. She had put all her hope and trust in him, she said, and with that she fell a'howling.

She sat there quite inconsolable, and rocked herself to and fro with all her hair over her eyes, till at last the drummer began to feel quite sorry for her and almost angry with himself. She was certainly most simple-minded and confiding.

All at once she twisted round and threw herself petulantly down from the haycock. Her eyes spied all about, and seemed quite tiny and piercing as she looked up at him, and laughed and jested.

He started back. It was exactly as if he again saw the snake beneath the birch tree down there when it trundled away.

And now he wanted to be off as quickly as possible; he cared no longer about being civil.

Then she reared up with a hissing sound. She quite forgot herself, and a long tail hung down and whisked about from behind her kirtle.

He shouldn't escape her in that way, she shrieked. He should first of all have a taste of public penance and public opinion from parish to parish. And then she called her father.

Then the drummer felt a grip on his jacket, and he was lifted right off his legs.

He was chucked into an empty cowshed, and the door was shut behind him.

There he stood and had nothing to look at but an old

billy goat through a crack in the door, who had odd, yellow eyes, and was very much like the old fellow, and a sunbeam through a little hole, which sunbeam crept higher and higher up the blank stable wall till late in the evening, when it went out altogether.

But towards night a voice outside said softly, "Swain! Swain!" And in the moonlight he saw a shadow cross the little hole.

"Hist! Hist! The old man is sleeping at the other side of the wall," it sounded.

He knew by the voice that it was she, the golden-red one, who had behaved so prettily and been so bashful the moment he had come upon the scene.

"Thou need'st but say that thou dost know that Serpent-eye has had a lover before, or they wouldn't be in such a hurry to get her off their hands with a dowry. Thou must know that the homestead westwards in the Blue Mountains is mine. And answer the old man that it was me, Brandi, that thou didst run after all the time. Hist! Hist! Here comes the old man," she whispered, and whisked away.

But a shadow again fell across the little hole in the moonlight, and the duck-necked one stuck her head in and peeped at him.

"Swain, swain, art thou awake? That Serpent-eye will make thee the laughing stock of the neighborhood. She's spiteful, and she stings. But the homestead westward in the Blue Mountains is mine, and when I play there the gates beneath the high mountains fly open, and through them lies the road to the nameless powers of nature. Do but say that 'twas me, Randi, thou wert running after, because she plays the *langelejk* so prettily. Hist, hist! The old man is stirring about by the wall!" she beckoned to him and was gone.

A little afterwards nearly every bit of the hole was

darkened, and he recognized the Black One by her voice.

"Swain, swain!" she hissed.

"I had to bind up my kirtle today behind," said she, "so we couldn't go dancing the *halling fling*[3] together on the green sward. But the homestead in the Blue Mountains is my lawful property, and tell the old man that it was madcap Gyri thou wast running after today, because thou art so madly fond of dancing jigs and *hallings*."

Then she clapped her hands aloud, and straightway was full of fear lest she should have awakened the old man.

And she was gone.

But the lad sat inside there, and thought it all over, and looked up at the thin pale summer moon, and he thought that never in his whole life had he been in such evil case.

From time to time he heard something moving, scraping, and snorting against the wall outside. It was the old fellow who lay there and kept watch over him.

"Thou, swain, thou," said another voice at the peephole.

It was she who had planted herself so firmly on the rock with such sturdy hips and such a masterful voice.

"For these three hundred years have I been blowing the *langelur*[4] here in the summer evenings far and wide, but never has it drawn anyone westward hither into the Blue Mountains. And let me tell thee that we are all homeless and houseless, and all thou seest here is but glitter and glamour. Many a man has been befooled hither time out of mind. But I won't have the other lasses married before me. And rather than that any one of them should get thee, I'll free thee from the mountains. Mark me, now! When the sun is hot and high the old man will get frightened and crawl into his corner. Then look to thy-

3. *Halling fling*: A country dance of a boisterous jig-like sort.
4. *Langelur*: A long wooden trumpet.

self. Shove hard against the door of the hayloft, and hasten to get thee over the fence, and thou wilt be rid of us."

The drummer was not slow to follow this counsel. He crept out the moment the sun began to burn, and cleared the fence with one good bound.

In less than no time he was down in the valley again.

And far, far away towards sunrise in the mountains, he heard the sound of her *langelur*.

He threw his drum across his shoulder, and hied him off to the maneuvers at Moen.

But never would he play rat-tat-tat and beat the tattoo before the lasses again, lest he should find himself westwards in the Blue Mountains before he was well aware of it.

"It's Me"

They had chatted so long about the lasses down in the valley and what a fine time they had of it there, that Gygra's[1] daughter grew sick and tired of it all, and began to heave rocks against the mountainside. She was bent upon taking service in the valley below, said she.

"Then go down to the ground gnome first, and grind thy nose down, and tidy thyself up a bit, and stick a comb in thy hair instead of an iron rake," said the dwellers in the mountains.

So Gygra's daughter tramped along in the middle of the river, till the channel steamed and the storm whirled round about her. Down she went to the ground gnome, and was scoured and scrubbed and combed out finely.

* * *

One evening a large-limbed coarse-grained wench stepped into the general dealer's kitchen, and asked if she could be taken into service.

"You must be cook, then," said Madame[2]. It seemed to her that the wench was one who would stir the porridge finely, and would make no bones about a little extra wood chopping and tub washing. So they took her on.

She was a roughish colt, and her ways were roughish too. The first time she carried in a load of wood, she shoved so violently against the kitchen door that she burst its hinges. And however many times the carpenter might mend the door, it always remained hingeless, for she burst it open with her foot every time she brought in wood.

1. *Gygra*: A giantess, the wife of the mountain gnome, who rules in the Dovrefeld.
2. Madame: I.e., the general's dealer's wife.

When she washed up, too, heaps and heaps of pots and pans were piled up higgledy-piggledy from meal to meal, so that the kitchen shelves and tables could hold no more, and bustle about as she might, they never seemed to grow less.

Nor had her mistress a much better opinion of her scouring.

When Toad, for so they called her, set to work with the sand brush, and scrubbed with all her might, the wooden, tin, and pewter vessels would no doubt have looked downright bonny if they hadn't broken to bits beneath her hands. And when her mistress tried to show her how it ought to be done, she only gasped and gaped.

Such sets of cracked cups, and such rows of chipped and handleless jugs and dishes, had never before been seen in that kitchen.

And then, too, she ate as much as all the other servants put together.

So her mistress complained to her master, and said that the sooner they were well quit of her the better.

Out in the kitchen went the general dealer straightway. He was quite red in the face, and flung open the kitchen door till it creaked again. He would let her know, he said, that she was not there to only stand with her back to the fire and warm her dirty self.

Now when he saw the lazy sluttish beast lounging over the kitchen bench and doing nothing but gape through the window panes at his boats, which lay down by the bridge laden with train-oil, he was downright furious. "Pack yourself off this instant!" said he.

But Toad showed her teeth, and grinned and blinked up at him, and said that as master himself had come into the kitchen, he should see that she did not eat his bread for nothing.

Then she slouched down to the boats, and snorted back

at him with her arm before her face. Before anyone could guess what she was after, she had one of the heavy hogsheads of train-oil on her back.

And back she came through the kitchen door, all smirking and smiling, and begged father to be so good as to tell her where she was to put it.

He simply stood and gaped at her. Such a thing he had never seen before.

And hogshead after hogshead she carried from the boat right up into the shop.

The general dealer laughed till he quite gasped for breath, and slapped his thighs so far as his big belly would let him reach them.

Nor was he sparing of compliments.

And into the dwelling room he rushed almost as quickly as he had rushed out of it.

"Mother has no idea what a capital wench she has got," said he.

But, ever after that, she put her hand to nothing, nay, not so much as to drive a wooden peg into the wall, and if someone else hadn't warmed up a thing or two now and then, there would have been very little to eat in the house. It was as much as they could do to get her away from the fireside at meal times.

When her mistress complained about it, her master said that she oughtn't to expect too much. The lass surely required a little rest now and again, after carrying such drayman's loads as she did.

But Toad always had an ogle and a grin ready at such times as the general dealer came through the door from the shop. Then she grew quick and lively enough, and went on all sorts of errands, whether it was with the bucket to the spring or to the storehouse for bread. And when she saw that her mistress was out of the way, she took it upon herself to do exactly as she liked, both in this

115

and in that.

No sooner was the pot hung on the pot hook, than she would slip away with a big saucer and fetch syrup from the shop. And she would flounce down before the porridge dish and gobble to her heart's content. If any of her fellow servants claimed an equal share, she would simply answer, "It's me!"

They dared not rebel. Since the day she had taken up the hogsheads of train-oil, they knew that she had master on her side.

But her mistress was not slow to mark the diminishing, both of the syrup pot and the powdered sugar, and she perceived also in which direction the gingerbreads and all the butter and bacon went. For out the wench would come, munching rye cakes and licking the syrup from her fingers.

And she grew as round and thick and fat as if she would burst.

When her mistress took away and kept the key, Toad would poke her head into the parlor door, and ogle and writhe at the general dealer, and ask if there was anything to carry up to the storeroom. And then he would go to the window and watch her as she lifted and carried kegs of fish and casks of sugar and sacks of meal.

He laughed till he coughed again, and, wiping the sweat from his forehead, would bellow all over the place: "Can any one of my laboring men carry loads like Toad can?"

And when her master came home, dripping wet and benumbed with cold, from his first autumn voyage, it was Toad who was first and foremost to meet him and unbutton his oilskin jacket for him, and undo his sou'wester, and help him off with his long sea boots.

He shivered and shook, but she was not slow to wring out his wet stockings for him, and fetch no end of birch

116

bark and huge logs. Then she made up a regular bonfire in the fireplace, and placed him cozily in the chimney corner.

Madame came to give her husband some warm ale posset, but she was so annoyed to see the wench whisking and bustling about him, that she went up into the parlor and howled with rage.

Early in the morning, the general dealer bawled and shouted downstairs for his long worsted stockings. They could hear that he was peevish and cross because he had to put on his sea jacket and cramped water boots, and go out again into the foul weather.

He tore open the kitchen door, and asked them furiously how much longer they were going to keep him waiting.

But now his mouth grew as wide open as the doorway he stood in, and his face quite lit up with satisfaction.

Round about the walls, and in the warmth of the chimney corner, hung his sou'wester, and his oilskin jacket, and his trousers, and every blessed bit of clothes he was to put on, as dry as tinder. And in the middle of the kitchen bench he saw his large sea boots standing there, so snug, and so nicely greased, that the grease ran right down the shafts and over the straps.

Such a servant for looking after him and taking care of him he had not believed it possible to get for love or money, cried the general dealer.

But now his wife could contain herself no longer. She showed him that the clothes were both scorched and burned, and that the whole of one side of the oilskin jacket was crumpled up with heat, and cracked if one pulled it ever so lightly.

And in she dragged the big butter keg, that he might see for himself how the wench had stuck both his boots in it and used it to grease them with.

But the general dealer stood there quite dumbfounded,

117

and glanced now at the boots and now at the butter tub.

He snapped his fingers, and his face twitched, and then he began to wipe away his tears. He hastened to go in that they might not see that he was weeping.

"Mother does not know how kindly the wench has meant it all," he sobbed. Good heavens! What if she *had* used butter for his boots, if she had only *meant* well. Never would he turn such a lass out of the house.

Then the wife gave it up altogether, and let the big kitchen wench rule as best she might. And it was not very long either before Toad let the key of the storeroom remain in the door from morn till eve. When anyone bawled out to her, "Who's inside there?" she would simply answer, "It's me!"

And she didn't budge from the gingerbread box, as she sat there and ate, even for Madame herself. But she always had an eye upon her master the general dealer.

But he only jested with her, and asked her if she got food enough, and said that he was afraid he would, one day, find her starved to death.

Towards Christmas time, when folks were making ready to go a-fishing, Madame was busy betimes and bustled about as usual, and got the great caldron taken down into the working room for washing and wool stamping.

The cooks hired for the occasion rolled out the *lefser*[3], and baked and frizzled on the flat oven pans. And they brought in herring kegs from the shop, and meal and meat, both cured and fresh, and weighed and measured, and laid in stores of provisions.

But then it seemed to Toad as if she hadn't a moment's peace for prying into pots and pans. Her mistress was going backwards and forwards continually, between storeroom and pantry, after meal, or sugar, or butter, or syrup for the *lefser*. The storeroom door was ajar for her all day

3. *lefser*: Thin cakes that can be doubled in two and eaten with syrup.

long.

So at last Toad grew downright wild. She was determined to put an end to all this racket. So she took it upon her to well smear the threshold of the storeroom with green soap.

Next morning her mistress came bustling along first thing with butter and a wooden ladle in a bowl, and she slipped and fell in the door opening between the stairs and the storehouse door.

There she lay till Toad dragged her up.

She carried her in to her husband with such a crying and yelling that it was heard all over the depot. Madame had been regularly worrying herself to death with all this bustle, said she, and now the poor soul had fallen and broken her leg.

But the one who cried the most, and didn't know what to do with himself when he heard such weeping and wailing over his wife, was the general dealer.

None knew the real worth of that kitchen wench, said he.

And so it was Toad who now superintended everything, and both dispensed the stores and made provisions for the household.

She drove all the hired cooks and pancake rollers out of the house—they were only eating her master out of house and home, she said.

The *lefser* were laid together without any syrup between them, and she gave out fat instead of butter. She distributed it herself, and packed it up in their *nistebommers*[4].

Never had the general dealer known the heavy household business disposed of so quickly as it was that year. He was quite astonished.

And he was really dumbfounded when Toad took him

---

4. *Nistebommers*: Boxes containing provisions for voyages or journeys.

up into the storeroom, and showed him how little had been consumed, and how the cured shoulders of mutton and the hams hung down from the rafters in rows and rows.

"So long as things went on as they were going now," said he, "she should have the control of the household like mother herself," for his wife was now bedridden in her room upstairs.

And at Yuletide Toad baked and roasted, and cut things down so finely that her fellow servants were almost driven to chew their wooden spoons and gnaw bones.

But such fat calves, and such ribs of pork, and such *lefser* filled with syrup and butter, and such *mölje*[5] and splendid fare for the guests that came to his house at Christmas time the general dealer had never seen before.

Then the general dealer took her by the arm, and right down into the shop they both went together.

She might take what she would, said he, both of kirtles and neckerchiefs and other finery, so that she might dress and go in and out as if she were mother herself, and she might provide herself with beads and silk as much as she liked. There was nothing that she might not have.

But when the bailiff and the sexton sat at cards, and Toad came in to lay the tablecloth, they were like to have rolled off their chairs. Such a sight they had never seen before. Toad had rigged herself up with all manner of party-colored 'kerchiefs, and trimmed her hairy poll with blue and yellow and green ribbons till it looked like a cart horse's tail. But they said nothing, for the sake of the general dealer, who thought she looked so smart, and was calling her in continually.

And they were forced to confess that the wench spared neither meat nor ale nor brandy. And on the third evening, when they got so drunk that they lay there like logs, she carried them off to bed as if they were sucking babes.

5. *mölje*: Flat cakes broken up and served with butter.

And so it went on, with feasting and entertaining, right up to the twentieth day after Christmas Day, and beyond it.

And that wench Toad used to smirk and stare about the room, and whenever they didn't laugh or jest enough with her, she would plant herself right in the middle of the floor, and turn herself about in all her finery to attract notice, and say, "It's me!"

And when the guests left the house they must needs admit that the general dealer was right when he said that such serving maids were not to be picked up every day.

But those folks who went fishing for the general dealer, and had their provisions put up for them beforehand, were not slow to mark that Toad had the control of the shop and stores likewise.

So it happened as might only have been expected. Their provisions ran short, and they had to return home just as the cod was biting best, while all the other fishermen sailed further out and made first-rate hauls.

The general dealer was like to have had apoplexy on the day that he saw his boats lying empty by the bridge in the height of the fishing season. His men came up in a body to the shop, headed by their eldest foreman, and laid a complaint before him.

The food that had been packed into their boxes and baskets, they said, couldn't be called human food at all. The *lefser* were so hard, they said, that it was munch munch all day; there was only rancid fat on them, with scarcely a glimpse of bacon, and as for the cured shoulders of mutton, one had scarcely shaved off a thin slice when one scraped against the bare bone.

Up into the storeroom went the general dealer like a shot.

But as for Toad, she smote her hands above her head, and said that it was as much as he, the general dealer, could manage, to meet the heavy expenses for fish hooks and fish baskets, and nets and lines, without having to provide his fishermen with salt herring and bacon, and fresh butter and *lefser* and ground coffee into the bargain. They had no need to starve when they had all the fish of the sea right under their noses, said she.

And then she handed him, as a specimen, one of his own *lefser*, which she had filled with butter and syrup herself, and let him taste it. And he tasted it, and ate and ate till the syrup ran down both corners of his mouth. Such good greasy *lefser* he had never tasted before.

Then the general dealer gave them a bit of his mind.

He was as red as a turkey cock, and out of the shop door they went head first—some three yards and some four, according as he got a good grip of them, and old Thore, who had steered the big *femböring*, both for him and his father, was discharged.

But Kjel, the herdsman, had hid himself out of the way up on the threshing floor whilst the row was going on, and the general dealer was shrieking and bellowing his worst in the yard below. And he stood there and peeped through the little window. Then he saw his mistress, who hadn't been out of bed for nine weeks, hobble forward and stare out of her bedroom window.

She took on terribly, and cried and wrung her thin hands when she saw their old foreman told to go to the devil, and shamble off with his cap in his hand as if he were deranged.

But she dared not so much as shout a word of comfort after him, for there stood Toad, big and broad, in the storehouse door, with a platter of *mölje* in her hand, and shook her fist after him.

Then Kjel was like to have wept too....That stout Toad should not grease herself shiny with *mölje* fat much longer in *their* house, or he'd know the reason why, thought Kjel.

And from thenceforth Kjel kept a strict watch upon her. There were lots of things going on that he couldn't make out at all.

Towards springtime, when they put the mast into the large new yacht which was to take the first trading voyage to Bergen, the general dealer was so glad that he was running up and down from the bridge to the house the whole day. He had never imagined that the yacht would have turned out so fine and stately.

And when they had the tackle and the shrouds all ready, and were hoisting away at the yards, he spun round on his heel and snapped his fingers—"That lass Toad should go with him to Bergen," said he. "She had never seen the town, poor thing! While as for mother, she had been there three times already."

But it seemed to Kjel that he saw more in this than other people saw.

As for Toad, when she heard she was to go to Bergen, she regularly turned the house upside down. There was nothing good enough for her in the whole shop; there was not a shelf that she didn't ransack to find the finery and frippery that glittered most.

And in the evening, when the others had lain them down to rest, she strolled over to the storehouse with a light.

But Kjel, who was a very light sleeper, was up and after her in an instant, and peeped at her through the crack in the door.

There he saw her cutting up the victuals and putting one tidbit aside after the other, *lefser* and sweetcakes and bacon and collared-beef, into the large chest which she had hidden behind the herring barrels. And on this, the last evening before their departure for Bergen, she had filled her provision chest so full that she had to sit upon it, with all her huge heavy weight, to press it down.

But the lock wouldn't catch; she had filled the chest too full, so she had to get up and stamp backwards on the lid till it regularly thundered, and sure enough she forced it down at last.

But the heel she stamped down upon it with was much more like the hoof of a horse than the foot of a human being, thought Kjel.

Then she carried the chest to the wagon that it might be smuggled on board without anyone seeing it. After that she went into the stable and unloosed the horse. But then there was a pretty to-do in the stable!

The horse knew that there was witchcraft afoot, and would not allow itself to be inspanned. Toad dragged and dragged, and the horse shied and kicked. At last the wench used her back legs, just as a mare does.

Such sport as that no human eye should have ever seen.

And straight off to the general dealer rushed Kjel, and got him to come out with him.

There in the moonshine that wench, Toad, and the dun horse were flinging out at each other as if for a wager, so that their hooves dashed against the framework of the stable door. Their long legs flew in turn over the stable walls, and the sparks scattered about in showers.

Then the general dealer grew all of a shiver and staggered about. Blood flew from his nose, and Kjel had to help him into the kitchen and duck his head in the sink. That night the general dealer didn't go to bed at all, but he walked up and down and stamped till the floor regularly thundered. And it was scarcely light next morning when he sent off Kjel with a dollar in his fist to old Thore the foreman. And he sent in the same way to all the boat people down by the shore.

Thore was told to put on his holiday clothes and get out the *femböring,* and row Madame herself to the yacht with the last lading. She should go with him to Bergen. There she should get both a silk dress and a shawl, and a gold watch and chain into the bargain, and engage a Bergen serving wench.

It was still early in the day when the yacht lay in the bay with her flag flying, all ready to start.

When they had hoisted the sail, that wench Toad, heavy and stout, came, puffing and blowing, across the bridge, in full parade, with rings on all her sprawling fingers, and her body covered with all the yellow and green and red ribbons she could possibly find room for on her ample person.

There she stood waiting for them to come back in the stately *femböring* and take her on board.

And when they began to raise the anchor, and the general dealer appeared on deck with his large meerschaum pipe and his telescope, she smirked and minced and wriggled and twisted, and cried aloud, "It's me!"

She thought he wanted to peep at her splendor through his spyglass.

All at once she saw Madame standing by his side in full traveling costume, and understood that they were going away without her.

Then she kicked out so that the planks of the bridge groaned and creaked beneath her. Right into the sea she plunged, and caught hold of the anchor, and tugged and held the ship back till the cable broke.

Then head over heels she went with both her hooves in the air.

But the yacht glided away under full sail, and the general dealer stood there and laughed till he nearly fell overboard.